"Did I _____ **hat costume** _____

A ghost _____ ght of the inn entrance she watched his expression. "No."

He gently ran a finger down her cheek. "Consider it said." Her warm breath brushed his finger as it caressed her lower lip. "You look like Little Red Riding Hood in that cape."

Jordon was a guest, and she shouldn't be standing here practically begging for his kiss. "You're beginning to look like the big bad wolf."

Jordon flashed a predatory grin and moved closer to her.

Excitement raced through her. "My, granny, what big eyes you have."

"Better to see you with my dear." He pushed her hood onto her shoulders.

"What big teeth you have, granny." Her breath stopped as he raised her chin.

"All the better to nibble on you, my dear." Jordon bent and tenderly captured her lower lip between his teeth.

Gretchen moaned with sweet, unexpected pleasure. She had been expecting a kiss, not this exquisite assault. Her hands clung to his back as she closed the gap between them. Frustration and desire made her bold. She wanted to taste him. She teasingly ran her tongue over his upper lip.

Jordon gave her what she wanted. He took her mouth in a kiss that promised wild nights and satisfied mornings. His hands pulled her closer as he leaned against the door and allowed her sweetness to wash over him. He wanted this woman, and he wanted her now. His snow angel was going up in flames in his arms. . . .

WHAT ARE *LOVESWEPT* ROMANCES?

They are stories of true romance and touching emotion. We believe those two very important ingredients are constants in our highly sensual and very believable stories in the *LOVESWEPT* line. Our goal is to give you, the reader, stories of consistently high quality that may sometimes make you laugh, sometimes make you cry, but are always fresh and creative and contain many delightful surprises within their pages.

Most romance fans read an enormous number of books. Those they truly love, they keep. Others may be traded with friends and soon forgotten. We hope that each *LOVESWEPT* romance will be a treasure—a "keeper." We will always try to publish

LOVE STORIES YOU'LL NEVER FORGET
BY AUTHORS YOU'LL ALWAYS REMEMBER

The Editors

Marcia Evanick

Gretchen and the Big Bad Wolf

BANTAM BOOKS

NEW YORK · TORONTO · LONDON · SYDNEY · AUCKLAND

GRETCHEN AND THE BIG BAD WOLF

A Bantam Book / April 1992

*If you would be interested in receiving protective vinyl
covers for your Loveswept books, please write to this address
for information:*

> *Loveswept
> Bantam Books
> P.O. Box 985
> Hicksville, NY 11802*

ISBN 0-553-44131-0

Published simultaneously in the United States and Canada

PRINTED IN THE UNITED STATES OF AMERICA

OPM   0 9 8 7 6 5 4 3 2 1

To my son, Keith—
who marches to a
different drummer.

Love,
Mom

"Men hang out signs indicative of their respective trades; Shoemakers hang out a gigantic shoe; Jewelers, a monster watch; and the Dentist hangs out a gold tooth. But up in the mountains of New Hampshire God Almighty has hung out a sign to show that there He makes men."

—DANIEL WEBSTER

One

Jordon Winters stared down at the limp thing cradled in his lap and cursed. This was definitely a first.

His glance shifted from the deflated airbag nestled across his thighs to the windshield and beyond. The dark blue hood of his car was half buried in a huge snowdrift. He had been cautiously driving down a snow-covered road, and within an instant he was kissing the high-tech plastic of an airbag. Owning a prestigious car had its privileges, such as smashing into an airbag instead of the steering wheel. But what was he supposed to do with the airbag now that it had collapsed?

Who in the hell would want to live in this tundra anyway? Well, maybe he was being a little harsh calling New Hampshire a frozen wasteland. The snow-covered mountains glistening in the late-afternoon light had held him enthralled until the blizzard had started.

Jordon looked out the snow-encrusted window

and stared down the deserted highway. He figured he was within walking distance of his destination, Edelweiss. With a rough twist he yanked the keys out of the ignition and unbuckled his seat belt. Walking a couple of miles in a blizzard without adequate attire didn't sound like fun, but it beat his other option. Spending the night in his car sounded suicidal.

He gazed at his briefcase, debating if he should take it with him, or lock it in the trunk, when the sound of sleigh bells echoed over the white landscape. Wondering if he had indeed hit his head on something, Jordon looked toward the sound. Amazed, he watched as a horse-drawn sleigh glided across the field in his direction. Currier and Ives had never painted anything like this.

Freezing wind and snow swirled around him as Jordon opened the door and stepped out to meet his rescuer.

Gretchen Horst pulled her coat hood lower over her face, trying to keep out Mother Nature's elements. She had been on the way back to the inn when she spotted the car half buried beneath a mound of snow. Since the road only led to one place, it was quite obvious to her that whoever was driving was either lost or going to Edelweiss. She squinted her eyes against the elements as a tall figure of a man emerged from the car. At least he wasn't stupid enough to try to walk. The road he was on twisted and turned for the next seven miles before ending at the heart of Edelweiss.

She maneuvered the horse and sleigh closer to the stuck car. Over the howl of the wind she yelled, "Need a lift?"

Jordon shaded his eyes and tried to get a better look at the person handling the sleigh. The voice that had been blown away by the wind had sounded feminine. Yards of green wool covered almost every inch of the driver's body. A bright red scarf was wrapped around the lower part of the face, and a hood was pulled over her forehead, leaving a small patch of space for breathing. The green bulk was either a female, or a male with a hormone problem. "Are you headed for Edelweiss?"

Gretchen heard the name of her town over the blustering wind. She dropped the reins and climbed down from her perch. The storm was building, they needed to get moving fast. "Anybody else with you?" She tried to see into the car.

"No."

"Luggage?"

"In the trunk." Now that he'd heard her speak a bit more, he decided she was female. As she walked past him, he gazed longingly at the massive boots on her feet. Wet, cold snow had seeped through his leather shoes. His toes were going numb standing there. He followed her to the trunk and opened it.

She reached in and hauled out the expensive garment bag and small suitcase, leaving the larger one. Jordon tried grabbing the suitcase from her, but was too late. She was already halfway back to the sleigh. The moving hulk had swung his garment bag's strap over her shoulder as if it contained cotton balls instead of thirty pounds of clothes. He quickly grabbed the larger case and his briefcase from the front seat, locked the car, and followed her footprints through six-inch-deep snow. After placing the cases in the back of the sleigh with the rest of his luggage, he climbed up next to the heap of green wool. "Thanks."

Her reply was muffled by the scarf and the wind, but he was pretty sure he heard something that sounded like "frozen tourists are bad for business."

Gretchen looked at the shivering man next to her and sighed. Why would anyone travel to New Hampshire in February in leather shoes, a suit, and a navy-blue top coat that was obviously meant for busy city streets, not a mountain road in wintertime? She reached under the seat and pulled out a thick blanket. "Wrap it around you."

Jordon gazed at the blanket. It looked like something the horse had worn. It also looked warm.

"Vanity could kill a man in this weather."

Was that a touch of laughter in her voice? He reached for the blanket, threw it over his shoulders, and pulled it around him. Vanity was clearly not one of her problems, unless the ugly coat and scarf hid a truly homely woman. By her size he guessed her favorite pastime was eating.

She handed him a bright-pink knit hat and a pair of matching mittens she had dug out of the deep pockets of her coat. Without hesitation he jammed the hat on his head and pulled it low over his hurting, reddened ears. The mittens barely warmed his numb fingers, but at least he was going to make it to his destination. Maybe it hadn't been such a good idea to wait until he reached Edelweiss to buy whatever outer gear he might need.

As the sleigh started to move, the bells on the harness gave off a pleasing sound. Jordon yanked up his collar against the wind and sank lower in the seat. He watched the expert way the woman handled the reins. Her red-gloved hands were petite, contrasting with the huge bulk of her body. "Are we near Edelweiss?"

Gretchen leaned closer to her passenger. "Less than a mile on this shortcut."

"Do you know where the Dragon's Lair is?"

She shot a glance at the man beside her. He should have looked ridiculous wearing her pink hat, but he didn't. He seemed like a man who did what had to be done. If putting on a silly pink hat kept his ears warm, by hell he was going to put one on.

Because of the fading light and weather conditions it was hard to tell what her passenger looked like, but she was certain who he was. Being the owner of the Dragon's Lair gave Gretchen the advantage—she knew who was coming and going. Her passenger was Jordon Winters, whose secretary didn't know how long her boss would be staying. "That's were I'm heading."

Jordon ducked his head as a vicious gust of wind seemed to penetrate every bone in his body. Lord, he was cold. Were all the studies, facts, and figures piled in his briefcase wrong? Who would want to live in this climate besides Nanook of the North? It looked like this trip had been for nothing.

A distant glimmer pulled his thoughts away from his discomfort. He shielded his eyes and looked ahead. They were approaching the town. Chalets beckoned with the warm glow of lights and smoke curling from chimneys. Not a soul was in sight as they jingled their way past what appeared to be the main square and headed for a huge, four-story chalet. A wooden sign, planted in front of the inn, blew wildly in the wind.

Gretchen expertly steered the sleigh to the rear of the inn. Well, it really didn't take any skill. Zelda knew exactly where she was, and where she wanted to go—to her nice, warm stall. Zelda wasn't anyone's fool. Gretchen halted the sleigh close to the back entrance as Gunter, her handyman, came dashing out the door.

Jordon was startled as rapid-fire German filled the air. From what he could gather, the old man seemed to be scolding his rescuer. Jordon climbed down and helped the woman out of the sleigh. Surprisingly she was extremely light on her feet.

"I'm sorry for upsetting you, Gunter. I know I'm late getting back." She took the blanket, hat and mittens Jordon handed her. "Could you see to Zelda while I take care of our guest, Mr. Winters?"

Muttering something in German, Gunter took the reins and led the horse and sleigh toward the barn.

"This way, Mr. Winters." She hurried to the door. "Gunter will bring in your luggage in a moment."

Jordon followed her into what appeared to be a cloakroom. Coats, boots, and skis were everywhere. He shook the snow out of his hair, unbuttoned his damp coat, and hung it on a peg. "How did you know my name?"

He turned to her and felt his mouth fall open. She had taken off the green coat and was now unzipping a red-and-yellow jacket. As she hung up the jacket, he saw a deep-purple sweater outlining a very feminine back. He swallowed hard when she bent over and unzipped knee-high boots. A curvy jean-clad bottom swayed slightly as she threw the boots onto the pile. She slipped her stocking-clad feet into a pair of loafers, pulled the red knit hat off her head, and fluffed her hair. Silver-blond hair tumbled to her waist.

Jordon wondered if he had fatally hit his head on the steering wheel. The vision standing in front of him had to be a snow angel who had guided him to heaven on her silvery sleigh. He had heard of the grim boatman, Charon, rowing the damned into hell, but never about sleigh rides into heaven.

Gretchen tossed her hat onto a shelf and turned to face her guest. "Welcome to the Dragon's Lair, Mr. Winters. I'm Gretchen Horst, the owner." She extended her hand. "If there's anything I can do for you, please just ask."

Clear, light-blue eyes sparkled under her golden brows. Her cheeks were flushed, and the cute, upturned nose was pink. A mouth made for kissing was smiling up at him. Definitely a snow angel. He took her hand and felt the chill of her fingers. "Can I buy you a drink for rescuing me?"

She released his warm fingers. "A brandy sounds like heaven. I'm sure a fire is going in the lounge. We can warm up in there."

Jordon had his own ideas about how to warm up, but he followed her out of the room anyway. He barely paid attention to the warm, friendly atmosphere of the registration area. His gaze was fastened to the gentle swaying of her hair and bottom as they stepped into the lounge and made their way to the blazing fire. He figured her to be around five foot five, nine inches shorter than his own six-foot-two frame. Was she married? She wasn't wearing a ring, but nowadays that didn't mean a thing.

"Mr. Winters?"

Jordon blinked and glanced around the rustic, restful lounge, finally noticing the knotty pine paneling and gleaming wooden floors. "I'm sorry, did you say something?"

Gretchen turned to the waiter waiting for their order. "We'll both take a brandy, Rutger." After the waiter hurried away, she said, "Why don't we sit down, Mr. Winters?" She studied his movements as he took the wing chair opposite her. "How long were you sitting in your car before I came?"

"Five minutes."

"Did you hit your head?" She gazed at his strong, handsome face, but couldn't detect any bruises. Maybe she should call a doctor just in case.

"No, the airbag prevented any injury."

"Do those things really work?" If she kept him talking for a few minutes maybe she could detect if he started to drift again. She did notice that his hair was drying into a lustrous black sheen.

Jordon accepted the glass of brandy from the waiter, who had returned with their drinks. "Amazingly, yes. I had my doubts too. That was until I ran into one of your snowdrifts."

"It wasn't *my* snowdrift." The dark gray of his eyes appeared normal. Were you supposed to allow an accident victim to drink? "Mother Nature doesn't allow you to own one of her miracles."

"You consider a snowdrift a miracle?"

"Anything Mother Nature does is a miracle." She lifted her glass to her lips and sipped. Warmth slipped into her stomach.

Jordon gazed at the moisture shimmering on her lips. The fire's light illuminated her complexion to a golden radiance. Would she taste like brandy? he wondered as liquid heat pooled in his body in places lower than his stomach. "Do you always know your guests' names?"

"We were expecting only a Jordon Winters and a Mr. and Mrs. Smythe."

"Ah, since I was alone and asked to be taken to the Dragon's Lair, you figured it out."

"No great mystery." She glanced around the room and smiled at the small gathering there.

Blizzards were great for the lounge business. She swirled her drink and relaxed in her chair. Jordon seemed perfectly normal with no side effects from the accident. "Gunter will have your bags in your room by the time you have registered."

Jordon looked down into the depths of his drink. He had completely forgotten about the briefcase. He should never have left it in the sleigh. In his line of business the less people knew, the smoother things went. The outcome always went his way regardless, but life was so much easier when it went smoothly. "That would be fine, Ms. Horst."

"Call me Gretchen." A friendly, though still professional smile curved her mouth. "We're very informal here."

He watched as a laughing couple strolled into the lounge. They looked as if they had just come off the slopes. Jeans and thick sweaters seemed to be the standard attire there. Framed poster-size photos of the Matterhorn and the Swiss Alps hung on the walls. Over the fireplace mantel was an ancient crossbow. Thankfully not one animal head adorned the place. There was something unnatural about trying to enjoy a drink while glass-eyed animals stared down at you. Gretchen obviously took Mother Nature very seriously. "I'll call you Gretchen"—he liked the way her name sounded on his tongue—"if you call me Jordon."

Her name had sounded deep and intimate the way he pronounced it. As if he were lying on rumpled sheets reaching for her. With a start Gretchen pulled her wicked imagination under control. Fantasies involving guests were strictly forbidden. Her mother had always said that one day her imagination would get her in trouble, and if her thoughts continued along these lines with Jordon, it surely would.

Gretchen quickly drank the rest of her brandy, but the heat coursing through her body had nothing to do with the liquor. She carefully placed the empty glass on the small table between the chairs. Time to get back to business. "Thank you for the offer of the drink, but these were on the house."

"But—"

"I needed to make sure you weren't suffering any ill-effects from the accident or exposure to the storm." She rose to her feet. "Have a pleasant stay in Edelweiss. As before, if I or any member of my staff can be of any assistance, please just ask."

Jordon's interested gaze followed Gretchen as she made her way through the lounge welcoming guests and being the cordial hostess. He knew a hasty retreat when he witnessed one; the only question was why? Maybe there was a husband somewhere. Hell, there might be half a dozen blond-haired children someplace too. Gretchen wasn't as young as she first appeared. He guessed she was about thirty-two. A very interesting, sexy, and tempting thirty-two.

He finished his drink, straightened his tie, and left the lounge to register. The sooner he secured his briefcase and started his business here, the more time he would have to make inquiries about one very alluring innkeeper.

Gretchen kept her expression friendly but not overly warm as she approached Jordon's table later that evening. "Mr. Winters, you wished to see me?"

Jordon stood up and smiled at the picture she made. A deep-purple flowing skirt with a multitude of yellow-and-pink flowers embroidered around the hem ended below her knees. A matching vest with equally talented stitchery was layered over a long-sleeved white silk blouse. Her hair had been pulled back into some type of intricate braid, and black leather dress boots covered her feet. Gretchen looked like her name—sweet, foreign, and innocent. "I thought you were going to call me Jordon?"

He had showered and changed. He looked more approachable and relaxed now, dressed in a thick gray sweater and black pants. His tie had been noticeably absent when he walked into the dining room less than an hour ago. "Was there something wrong with your dinner . . ." She hesitated a brief moment before adding, ". . . Jordon?"

The fifty-minute wait had been worth it just to hear her say his name. "No, dinner was superb. The dessert is going to cause me the problems."

A frown creased her brow. "Oh?"

"I seem to have ordered too much." A discreet inquiry at the front desk proved she was indeed single and unattached. The clerk had been very helpful when she confided that the Dragon's Lair was Gretchen's life.

Gretchen saw the invitation coming a mile away and wanted to avoid the scene. Many a night she had joined guests over dessert or drinks to discuss the skiing conditions, the slopes, or just the weather. She enjoyed the company of groups, couples, and even the occasional single male, but there was something about Jordon that shouted *danger*. He was entirely too tempting for her peace of mind. "I'm sorry but I—"

"Oh, good, Ms. Horst, you decided to join Mr. Winters."

Gretchen turned toward the approaching waiter

and bit back a silent groan. Peter was holding a tray containing dessert for two. It would cause more trouble than it was worth to refuse now. She was a mature woman of thirty-two; if she couldn't sit down for dessert with an attractive man and not fantasize about his body, she was in sad shape.

Jordon saw the acceptance in her eyes and quickly moved around the table and pulled out the chair. "Peter was very helpful. He recommended your favorite, the chocolate cake."

Gretchen smiled her thanks to the beaming Peter as he placed the dessert and extra coffee cup on the table.

Jordon waited until the waiter had gone to comment, "I usually don't bulldoze innkeepers into having dessert with me."

If she didn't stop eating Effie's delicious desserts, they would have to widen the doorways throughout the inn. "What do you usually do?"

"Ask the woman to join me for dinner."

"You tried that already when you came downstairs earlier. If I'm not mistaken, I explained that I act as hostess while the dining room is open." She took a small bite of cake and savored the rich taste. If she set her imagination on Effie's cake, maybe she wouldn't notice the single dimple that appeared on the left side of Jordon's mouth whenever he smiled. Business and pleasure went together as well as chocolate and her waistline. One was always disastrous for the other.

"I had to do something for you."

Gretchen raised a pale eyebrow. "Oh?"

"You saved my life." Her exquisite laughter washed over him. "Okay, maybe not saved it, but you did save me a very long, cold walk."

Gretchen stopped laughing. "You weren't planning on leaving your car and walking, were you?"

"I wasn't looking forward to it, believe me."

"Don't you know that you are never to leave your car in the middle of a blizzard?"

"The prospects of freezing my tail off all night in a stuck car far outweighed the dangers of a walk of a couple of miles."

She placed her fork down and stared at Jordon in horror. "Not only weren't you properly dressed for a snowstorm, but the road you were on curved and swirled its way around the mountain for seven miles before reaching Edelweiss."

Jordon flashed a provocative smile. "Then I owe you a double thank you. I would have been frozen solid by the time I reached the Dragon's Lair."

Gretchen shook her head at the foolhardiness and mumbled, "If you would have made it at all."

A spark of steely determination smoldered in his gray eyes. "I would have made it, Gretchen."

She cautiously took a sip of coffee and studied her guest. For some unknown reason she believed him. If Jordon Winters set out to walk seven miles through a snowstorm, he would make it. Unnerved by his raw conviction, she shifted her attention back to the delicious dessert. "Do you come to New England a lot?"

"I was in Vermont for a weekend a couple of years ago."

"Skiing?"

"No, it was during the fall. I'm afraid I gravitate toward warmer weather."

She smiled at his confession. Not many people would admit they preferred the beach, sun, and fun to an innkeeper in New Hampshire who depended on the winter tourism for her livelihood. "What brings you to Edelweiss if not the slopes?"

Jordon carefully tasted the coffee. This was one

subject he had wanted to avoid for the time being. In a couple of days everyone would know what he was doing here. But in the meantime he wanted to appraise the situation and his opponents. The report he had stated that Edelweiss was the perfect location for the condominiums his company built. The drawbacks were the town's council and some thick-headed mayor who insisted that Edelweiss not grow. There were always stumbling blocks in every project. Jordon usually left it up to his employees to move those blocks, except this time. He was bored with sitting in his New York office while his staff hoisted, pushed, or bought away those blocks. He needed a challenge. He was hoping that getting personally involved with a project again would relieve his discontent.

He raised his gaze and encountered her curious glance. "I needed a challenge."

She paled. "Not Suicide Pass!"

Intrigued, he asked, "What's that?"

Gretchen relaxed. If he didn't know what it was, he wasn't here to conquer it. "It's a ski trail that only the foolhardy attempt."

"Or the most experienced?"

"Even the best can't win when Mother Nature decides to enter the race, Mr. Winters." She forced her thoughts away from unpleasant memories and asked, "What type of challenge are you looking for?"

Jordon nearly said, *Uncovering the reason behind the sadness that has just darkened your eyes,* but didn't. He knew some challenges were better kept unspoken. "I'll start with a little one"— his dimple flashed—"such as learning to ski."

Gretchen chuckled. "Sorry about that. We have an excellent beginner's class at Donner Mountain."

"*Donner* Mountain?"

"Thunder Mountain. The Swiss immigrants who first settled here named it Thunder Mountain because of the fierce rumblings that seem to vibrate and bounce off it."

"Is it thunder?"

"It's either the echoes of thunder or the distant roar of the mountain dragons." Seeing Jordon's bemused expression, she chuckled. "In Switzerland they still pass down through generations the legends and stories of dragons. Fire-breathing mountain dwellers lived throughout the Alps and fed off stray cattle and lost children."

"Charming bedtime story."

"When they came to America, they thought they were safe from the dragons. So when the rumbling started, they stubbornly named the mountain Donner Mountain."

"And started a ski school."

"The skiing came later. The first settlers were more interested in making a living than in the relaxing sports of skiing and mountain climbing."

"You can climb Thunder Mountain?"

"If you're experienced enough, they have guided climbs up the difficult northern slope during the summer months." She finished the remaining cake.

"Did anyone ever encounter a dragon?"

"I'm sure I would have heard if they had."

He noticed the way her eyes sparkled and laughed when she talked about the dragons. "Why did you name the inn the Dragon's Lair?"

"How did you know I named it?"

Jordon noticed the gleam of surprise in her eyes. Gretchen was as easy to read as a book. All he had to do was look into her eyes. "It seemed like something you would do."

"What can I say. I spent too many hours on my grandmother's knee absorbed in spellbinding tales."

"What I haven't been able to figure out is why I haven't seen any dragons in the inn?"

"Oh, but there is one *very* large dragon here."

The way she said the word *very* led him to believe it must be huge. "Where?"

"Only a handful of people have spotted it, and no one has understood it yet."

"Now *I'm* curious." Jordon was trying to figure out how to gather some clues as to where the beast was when a harried-looking man rushed up to their table.

"Gretchen, here you are," he said with a thick German accent. He then turned to Jordon and apologized. "I'm sorry for interrupting."

"It's okay, Hans, what is it?" Gretchen's voice was friendly and smooth.

"It's Claus again. He was visiting all the shops today trying to pressure the owners into voting against the council."

Jordon studied the man more closely.

"Hans, I told you before, the business owners cannot vote against the town council. The council is unanimous in its decision, and next Tuesday night we vote that William Tell's statue stays in the center of town, where it has been for years."

Jordon heard the *we vote* and frowned. Sweet, charming Gretchen was on the town council.

"But he's telling everyone it's un-American and that that's why business is so bad."

"Hans, you know that's not true, and I'm sure the other owners are aware that Edelweiss's problems don't stem from the fact that we have a statue of a Swiss folk hero in our town square."

Jordon smiled in relief and reached for his

coffee. Sweet, intelligent Gretchen was level-headed. The reports of the stubbornness of the town council had to be exaggerated. This trip to Edelweiss wasn't going to be a challenge after all. He gazed at the luscious curve of Gretchen's mouth. But, then again . . .

Hans wrung his hands and pleaded, "Please, Gretchen, don't let them take down the statue."

"No one is going to take down Willie's statue, Hans." She smiled reassuringly at the man. In a voice that brooked no argument she said, "Not while I'm the mayor of this town."

Jordon choked on his coffee. Sexy, alluring Gretchen, whom he had been fantasizing about since she had taken off her coat was the thick-headed mayor of Edelweiss. She was the one he came to hoist, push, or buy out of his company's way. His snow angel was blocking a multi-million-dollar deal!

Gretchen glanced quickly at Jordon to see if he was all right.

Hans worshipfully beamed at the mayor of Edel-weiss.

Two

Jordon stood in his room and stared through the glass doors into the night. The charming town of Edelweiss was spread out two stories below. The storm had finally tapered off into a light flurry. Old-fashioned streetlights beamed their welcome across the newly fallen snow. Nothing moved except the scattering of flakes dancing on the wind. Not a sound reached his ear. Edelweiss was definitely not New York City. A blizzard would not have stopped his hometown. Only a blackout had been known to grind his city to a halt.

Jordon glanced at his watch before returning his gaze to the tranquil scene outside. One-thirty in the morning. The village of Edelweiss was asleep. His city never slept.

He turned away from the glass doors that led to a small snow-covered balcony and frowned at the piles of papers spread out across the bed and table, spilling over onto the carpet. He rubbed the bridge of his nose and tried to remember which pile he had been reading when he had laid his glasses down. Facts, figures, and ordinances jumbled together in his head to be mixed with the image of clear, intelligent blue eyes. Gretchen's eyes.

Edelweiss's building codes applied not only to the actual town but to the surrounding area. When the first Swiss immigrants built the town, they wanted it to resemble their homeland as much as possible. Thirty years ago, when tourism started to become a major factor, a couple from the city wanted to build a modern vacation home, and the surrounding area had been quickly added to the building ordinance. Edelweiss was to be kept uniquely Swiss.

Jordon had to change not only the mayor's mind but also the six other members of the town council. He put on his glasses and studied the bottom figure printed on the computer printout in his hand. Building fifty practical high-rise condominiums at the foot of Shadow Mountain would net his company a substantial profit. If he were forced to build fifty authentic Swiss chalets, he would be stuck with them. He would need more property since the chalets couldn't be stacked, and the authentic touches would mean a higher price—and more upkeep for the owners. The people who could afford to plop down a quarter million for a condo for a winter home wanted a hassle-free home where they could relax and enjoy life. Not someplace where they had to worry about year-round landscaping and maintenance. Condominiums were where the money was. It was about time Edelweiss woke up and joined the twentieth century.

Jordon removed his glasses and transferred the papers on his bed to a table. He quickly stripped, turned off the lights, and slipped under the heavy quilt. He wondered what Edelweiss's sexy mayor was doing that very moment. Was she snuggled up under some quilt wearing flannel pajamas, or was the quilt the only thing keeping her warm? His eyes adjusted to the darkness as he crossed his arms under his head and stared up at the ceiling. Jordon knew sleep would be a long time coming.

Gretchen continued her conversation with Jarvis as the first customer of the day stepped into his shop. Her back was to the door, racks of coats and pants, and shelves overflowing with expensive hand-knitted sweaters. Jarvis's exclusive men's shop was at the heart of Edelweiss and was conveniently located next door to his wife's boutique. "I know you're upset about your son deciding not to return to Edelweiss after graduating from college. A lot of children don't settle down where they grew up."

Jarvis shook his gray head and pulled on his beard. His stout figure and the highly decorated red vest gave him the appearance of an elf instead of a store owner. "That may be true, Gretchen, but in Edelweiss no children settle where they were raised. Edelweiss holds no future for its young."

Gretchen frowned and chewed on her lower lip. Jarvis was right. How could she argue with the truth? She had been one of the young who finished college and went looking for greener pastures. She had found them in a rapidly growing hotel chain based in San Francisco. With hard work, intelligence, and the desire to succeed, she had worked her way up the rungs of the corporate ladder, only to discover it contained termites. Gretchen had returned to safe, secure Edelweiss five years ago disillusioned and mistrustful of the outside world.

Today she stood firm and strong against any outside influences over Edelweiss. When she was elected mayor two years ago, she had vowed to keep the village unique and safe. She had kept that promise. Edelweiss was unique and safe, but it was apparent it wasn't thriving. It couldn't support the young who wanted to start families and raise them in the same way they had been raised. Edelweiss was dying before her eyes, and she didn't know how to help it. "You're right, Jarvis." She jammed her hand into the pockets of her ski jacket. "We have more important things to worry about than Willie's statue."

Jarvis glanced at the customer looking at a down-filled ski jacket. He started around the counter. "Did you find out anything?"

"No, the Beckers are being very tight-lipped."

"You think they are selling?"

Gretchen pictured the Beckers' farm in her mind and sighed. It was a gorgeous piece of property. One hundred and sixty-two acres of rolling pastures at the foot of Shadow Mountain overlooking the village of Edelweiss. "I don't know, Jarvis. I get the feeling they still blame Edelweiss for driving off their sons."

Jarvis snorted. "Those two boys were trouble from day one. I say good riddance." He headed over to help his customer.

Gretchen turned and watched as he walked away. Surprise brightened her eyes when she saw who the customer was. Jordon Winters was busily trying on jackets. She leaned against the counter and admired the view. The man did possess one pair of fine-looking buns. Gretchen scolded herself as she forced her eyes upward. Trim waist, broad shoulders, and gleaming thick black hair only enhanced her initial opinion. Jordon Winters was intriguing enough for her to break her own rules about not mixing business with pleasure. Last night after dessert she had been bewildered when he graciously paid the check and disappeared. She had been hoping for an invitation for drinks. He had been telling the truth when he said he only wanted to thank her for saving him a long, cold walk. In the light of the morning she was thankful he hadn't issued any invitation. If her dreams from last night were any indication, it had been a long time since she had mixed pleasure with anything.

Jordon felt Gretchen's gaze and glanced over his shoulder. A delicate pink blush swept up her cheeks. A devilish smile teased the corners of his mouth. *My snow angel blushes.* He turned back to the shopkeeper and studied the two jackets in his hand. "Let's get a second opinion." He held up the jackets and pinned Gretchen with a challenging look. "Which one, Ms. Horst?"

Gretchen hid her surprise at being asked. Choosing a man's clothes seemed so intimate. She eyed the navy-and-maroon jacket. It was obviously expensive, refined, and boring. It was also the one Jordon seemed to favor. She looked at the other jacket and grinned. Canary yellow and black radiated a sense of adventure and fun. The man who wore that jacket was her kind of man. Tempting the fates, she pointed to the yellow-and-black jacket. "That one."

Jordon frowned and stared at the jacket. If he wore that, he wouldn't have to worry about plowing people down on the slopes. They would see him coming a mile away and run for their lives. He would look like a demented bumblebee. He looked at the beaming clerk and then back at the jacket. He had never owned anything canary yellow before, let alone worn it. He handed the plain dark jacket to the clerk. "I'll take that one." He glanced at Gretchen. Was that disappointment that flashed across her face? "I'm not a yellow person."

"My loss," Gretchen muttered.

"Pardon?"

"Nothing." She cleared her throat. "If you're planning on learning to ski, you'd better have Jarvis outfit you properly." She pushed away from the counter and headed for the door. "I might not be around to lend you my hat and mittens again."

Jordon realized she was leaving. "Why don't you stick around and make sure I get everything?"

"I can't. I have some business to take care of."

"I thought frozen tourists were bad for business."

Gretchen chuckled and opened the door. "Jarvis, make sure Mr. Winters is well equipped to handle anything a New Hampshire winter can throw at him." She stepped out onto the newly shoveled walk and closed the door behind her.

Jordon glanced down at the yellow-and-black jacket still in his hand. Why did Gretchen leave in such a hurry? He had shopped for clothes a couple of times with a member of the opposite sex. When he had chosen something that didn't suit their taste, they pouted prettily or started on some nonsense about certain colors bringing out the color of his eyes, obviously thinking that compliments would sway him. Gretchen had done neither. She had honestly been upset because he picked the darker jacket and not because he went against her choice. He looked at the discreet price tag. The one he had picked was more expensive. So why had she been disappointed?

"Mr. Winters, if you would be so kind as to follow me."

Jordon hung the brightly colored jacket back up and followed the older man to the rack of snow pants.

By the time Jordon replaced his credit card in his wallet, the shopkeeper looked in shock. Not only had he purchased the coat and pants but several trousers and sweaters. It looked as if he was staying in Edelweiss for some time. He might as well try to fit in with their relaxed manner. "Could you please have everything delivered to the Dragon's Lair? I have a couple of other stops I want to make, or I would take them with me."

"Yes, sir, Mr. Winters." Jarvis peered at the towering stack of boxes and bit back a grin.

"Thank you, Jarvis." Jordon knew he should have tried to pump some information out of Jarvis, but he couldn't bring himself to do it. He didn't want to trick one of the members of the town's council. Besides, the man looked as if he baked cookies in an ancient oak tree.

Jordon headed out onto the street and was amazed by the speed with which Edelweiss had dug herself out from under yesterday's blizzard. Streets and sidewalks were clear. All the shops were open and beckoned tourists to come and explore. The only problem Jordon could detect was that there weren't any tourists. The town seemed empty.

He walked past a women's apparel shop and stopped to gaze into a clockmaker's window. An assortment of intricate cuckoo clocks lined an entire wall inside the shop. It was a crime to let this beautiful shop stand empty. His condominiums would boost the economy. Who knows, maybe Edelweiss would become the eastern version of Aspen. The Dragon's Lair would be over-flowing with tourists, the assorted bed and breakfasts throughout town would be booked solid, and the shops would be flooded with customers. How could the mayor or the council argue against such resounding odds?

Jordon stepped into the next shop, the florist. He would make Edelweiss see reason with their own pocketbooks. His job in the village would be over with before the week was out. He ordered a dozen long-stemmed yellow roses to be delivered to Gretchen. With business coming to a rapid close he might just stay an extra week and take a real vacation.

Gretchen rearranged the roses for the third time. It had been a long while since anyone had sent her flowers. If her warm, light-hearted feeling was any judge, it had been too long. She glanced down at the card on the coffee table. Jordon's handwriting was like him, strong and bold. She frowned as she reread the message for the seventh time: *Is yellow your favorite color? Join me for dessert again, please."* He had signed the note with a bold "J."

She walked through the office connecting her fourth-floor apartment with the inn's storage room and took the service elevator down. She was going to be late if she didn't hurry.

She dashed into the inn's kitchen and smiled at the chaos. Everything was running smoothly. Effie was in control. Gretchen always told herself that the day she entered the kitchen to find everything neat, orderly, and quiet was the day she'd panic. Tonight was not that night. "Hi, Effie. Everything all right?"

"Ja, fine, fine." Effie moved her bulk with considerable grace and pulled a batch of apple dumplings from the oven. Gretchen's mouth started to water. She knew she shouldn't have stepped foot into the kitchen while Effie was around.

Peter rushed into the kitchen. "Peter, I need you to do me a favor."

He skidded to a halt in front of her. "Sure, Ms. Horst, what is it?"

She quickly scribbled a note on the back of a napkin. "Do you remember Mr. Winters from last night?" At his nod she handed him the note. "Is he in the dining hall?"

"Yes, Ms. Horst. He's eating right now."

"Could you please give him this note?"

Peter smiled shyly, but made no comment as he hurried back out into the dinning hall. Gretchen debated peering through the dining room's door to see Jordon's expression when he learned she wouldn't be joining him tonight, but decided against it. He was entirely too tempting, and everyone knew Gretchen's self-control rated up there with world peace. There was none.

She quickly grabbed a plate and reached for a steaming apple dumpling and a fork. Gretchen made it halfway out the door before Effie noticed the theft and spouted a stream of German strong enough to blister an innocent's ear. Gretchen was thankful she had outgrown the innocent stage years ago, because what Effie was suggesting was a physical impossibility.

Jordon entered the boisterous hall and grimaced. His snow angel was in this crush somewhere? Streamers, balloons, and glittery silver snowflakes hung from the ceiling. Rows of tables were packed with tourists and residents of Edelweiss clapping wildly, guzzling beer, and devouring sausage sandwiches. A dance floor had been cleared near the band, and a group of villagers were dressed in native Swiss costumes demonstrating a folk dance. He glanced around the crowded room looking for Gretchen.

When Peter had handed him the note from Gretchen, disappointment had shot through him. After reading the brief message, *Sorry, can't join you this evening, it's Wednesday. Gretchen. P.S. The flowers are so beautiful, I just might change my favorite color to yellow.*, he became curious. What happened on Wednesday? He finished his dinner and glanced around the nearly deserted dining hall. Something was definitely happening somewhere. Where was everyone? After a few pointed questions to the hostess, he ended up at the local firehouse's banquet hall for the weekly folk festival.

Jordon watched in amusement as the dancers, who had been kicking up their heels, pulled tourists onto the floor and started to teach them some steps. A buxom waitress, dressed in traditional garb, thrust a tankard of beer into his hands. Before he could utter his thanks, she had skillfully skirted away to another empty-handed customer. Edelweiss was throwing a keg party!

He slowly worked his way around the crowd, heading toward the kitchen, hoping to spot Gretchen. A deep chuckle escaped his throat as a group of men exchanged jokes of questionable taste. The courteous residents of Edelweiss were translating the punchlines into graphic and easily understandable German. There was something comical about men dressed in knickers, knee socks, and suspenders sharing dirty jokes. They all looked like deranged escapees from an English prep school.

A burst of feminine giggles caught his attention. A group of women were clustered in a corner obviously discussing some of the merits of the gentlemen dancers. Gretchen wasn't among them. He leaned against the wall and sipped his beer. The hostess must have been wrong. Gretchen wasn't here.

He had resigned himself to the evening without her company when he spotted a silver-blond halo. Jordon moved through the throng and froze in astonishment when he saw her. Gretchen's hair was braided and wrapped in a crown around her head with half a dozen daisies interwoven throughout. She was wearing a high-necked ruf- fled white blouse, deep purple floor-length skirt with an equally long golden apron tied around her waist. Some type of black vest was over the blouse, but he couldn't see it too well. It was hidden by the most bizarre object—an accordion. His sweet, sexy snow angel was playing an accor- dion.

Jordon watched transfixed as her fingers flew over the keyboard while her left hand pressed buttons and squeezed the box in and out. Her laughter at something the horn player had said reached him halfway across the room. She was thoroughly engrossed in the music and the fun. Her toes were tapping, and her enticing hips were seductively swaying to the beat. Heat clawed at his gut. *He wanted her.* He wanted the passion she was pouring into the music to be directed at him. Lord, help him, he wanted a woman who played the accordion.

With a hasty gulp of beer he backed up and found an empty seat at a table within sight of the band. The desire burning in his gut surprised him. Why Gretchen? He had made love to more beautiful and sophisticated ladies in his past. There shouldn't have been one thing seductive about Gretchen tonight. She was covered from neck to toe in garments that went out of fashion over a hundred years ago. She was half hidden and playing one of the most unglamorous instruments ever invented. Everything about her should have been a turnoff. So why was he sitting here wondering how to get her into his bed?

Jordon frowned and drained the tankard. He couldn't make love to her. She was the mayor of Edelweiss. She was the stumbling block on a million-dollar deal. She was business, and he'd never mixed business with pleasure. She had eyes the color of noontime skies over Tahiti. She was going to be trouble. Hell, she was already trouble. Jordon signaled the waitress for another beer.

Gretchen spotted Jordon through the crowd and missed two notes. No one noticed. Her accordion playing was mediocre at best. Hilda, the band's usual player, was at home eight months pregnant. Gretchen had been railroaded into filling in until the baby was born. What Gretchen lacked in talent, she made up for in enthusiasm. The weekly folk festivals during winter months had been her idea two years ago, and they had somewhat helped boost the tourist industry. The town had always been willing to follow her lead. They looked up to her and expected her to have all the answers. Lord, how she wished she did.

When she returned to Edelweiss five years ago, the town was on a rapid downhill slide. She must have seemed like a heroine waltzing back into town, purchasing the neglected inn, and sinking everything she had into the Dragon's Lair. Little did the town realize she was running scared of the outside world. Her concern for Edelweiss stemmed from necessity, not heroics. She needed Edelweiss to survive. Over the years she had sunk her heart and soul into the village, and in return they had given her respect, love, and the dubious honor of being their mayor. Every season it was becoming harder and harder to keep Edelweiss stable. The village hadn't prospered under her guidance, but then it hadn't slipped into the black hole known as bankruptcy either.

Gretchen sneaked another peek at Jordon. He was sitting by himself staring into his glass of beer. No one could accuse him of being the life of the party. Why had he bothered to come if he wasn't going to participate in the fun? Take away his heartbreak body, the peek-a-boo dimple, and his deep, smooth voice that hinted at wild nights and satisfied mornings and he would definitely not be her type.

She watched as Hans and Gunter sat down next to Jordon. Within moments the three were laughing and talking like long-lost friends. So, he can be social! It didn't change anything; he still wasn't her type. So why had her heartbeat increased as soon as she had spotted him?

Gretchen had started in on the last number of the set when her fingers slipped across the keyboard, causing three members of the band to lose the melody. Greta and Giselle, the looking-for-a-rich-husband twins of Edelweiss, had zeroed in on Jordon. Both were twenty-two, beautiful, and blond. Every time Hans saw them together, he became homesick for his native Switzerland. The general consensus among the male population was that when the two stood side by side, their chests rivaled the Alps.

Gretchen finished the song and frowned down at her chest as she placed the accordion on the floor. The Alpine twins could never play the accordion.

"Can I buy you a drink?"

Surprised, Gretchen quickly spun around and nearly knocked Jordon over. He grabbed her shoulders to steady her. She was breathless as she said, "Sorry, I didn't see you standing there."

Jordon reluctantly removed his hands. "I saw the band was about to take a break, and I wanted to make sure I was the first one here."

Gretchen shot a quick glance over at the table where he had been sitting. Greta and Giselle were pouting, Hans was busy being homesick, and Gunter was looking back at her with a knowing expression. Jordon had to have flown across the room to make it to the band area in such a short time. He made it sound as if hordes of males were lining up for the chance of buying the local accordion player a beer. She gazed around. They were the only ones left standing by the instruments. "I don't drink and play. The accordion could become a lethal weapon to a drunk." She saw a frown pulling at his mouth. "But I would love a cold soda."

"You're on." He placed his hand on her back and propelled her through the crowd to his table. Her leather vest felt soft and supple under his hand. White laces criss-crossed their way up from her slim waist to form a tempting bow on the upper slopes of her breasts. His fingers itched to untie that delicate bow. "I imagine playing the accordion could build a thirst."

Gretchen glanced over her shoulder at him. "Try sore shoulders and back."

Jordon grinned devilishly. "I give a wicked massage."

"I'll keep that in mind," she said as she sat down next to Hans. Jordon's dimple had pulled a sneak attack on her heart. She wanted to cry *foul* against such an underhanded maneuver. The man was becoming impossible to resist.

Gretchen looked at the flush on Hans's face. "How's it going, Hans?"

His gaze never leaving the Alpine twins, Hans replied, "Mountain climbing."

Gunter chuckled, and Jordon turned a curious shade of red and excused himself to get Gretchen's drink. The twins never caught on to the meaning.

By the time Gretchen had to return to the band area, her opinions of Jordon had gone another hundred-and-eighty-degree turn. The man not only possessed a keen sense of humor and the uncanny ability to pick up German, but he had politely ignored the gorgeous twins and focused his attention on her. The man was sending out signals, loud and clear. He was interested.

Two hours later Gretchen packed away the accordion and bid the other members of the band good night. The only other people around were a handful of kitchen help, a lone man stacking chairs in the corner, and Jordon. He had waited. Gretchen picked up the case and headed for the door.

"I'll take that."

Gretchen smiled up at Jordon. "I'm only putting it in the closet."

"Aren't you taking it home?"

"No, it's not mine. It's Hilda's, the real accordion player. I'm only filling in temporarily."

Jordon eyed the case. "I've never carried anyone's accordion before."

She opened the closet door and shoved the case behind a box of Styrofoam cups and a gross of white tissue paper. "Were you one of those boys who always carried some girl's books home from school?" She reached for the floor-length red cape on a hanger.

Jordon helped her on with the cape. "Afraid not. I went to an all-boys' school." He put on his jacket. "Do you do this every Wednesday?"

"Only during the winter months." She slipped on a pair of gloves and pulled up the hood as they stepped out into the blustery cold. "During the rest of the year the festivals are held in the park."

Jordon turned up his collar and jammed his hands into his pockets. "Aren't you afraid someone will get drunk and drive his car off some mountain?"

"The women's auxiliary keeps track of who's drinking and how much." Gretchen chuckled. "I bet if I ask Eva how many beers you had, she could tell me to the ounce. Besides, didn't you notice?"

"Notice what?"

"No one drove. There wasn't one car in the parking lot. Everyone walks to the festival. No one wants to be the designated driver, and secondly it takes longer for your car to heat up than it does to walk home."

Jordon glanced behind them. The firehouse had faded into the distance. The warm glow of the Dragon's Lair lights could be seen ahead. The glaring differences between just a dot on a map of Edelweiss and the sprawling metropolis of New York rocked his mind. It was a little past eleven, and they were the only two people on the street. It was as if they had been transported to another country, hell, another planet. "Is it always so quiet around here?"

Gretchen drew her cape tighter around her and hurried up the walk to the inn. "Of course. It's one of the things we pride ourselves on. Peace, quiet, snow, and the leisurely pace to enable us to appreciate the wonders of Mother Nature."

Jordon stopped her hand as it was reaching for the doorknob. If they walked into the inn, Gretchen would be pulled away by some kind of business, or another guest would demand her attention. "Did I mention how wonderful you look in your costume?"

A smile touched her lips. In the pale glow of the entrance lights she watched his expression. "No."

He rose his hand and gently ran his finger down her icy cheek. "Consider it said." Her warm breath brushed across his finger as it caressed her lower lip. "You look like Little Red Riding Hood in that cape."

The heat seeping into her bones couldn't be credited to the way the inn was blocking the wintery blasts of frigid air. But Jordon was a guest, and she should definitely not be standing here practically begging for his kiss. "You're beginning to look like the big bad wolf."

Jordon flashed a predatory grin and moved in closer.

Excitement raced through her body. "My, Granny, what big eyes you have."

"The better to see you with, my dear." He pushed her hood back onto her shoulders.

"What big teeth you have, Granny." Her breath stopped as he tilted up her chin.

"All the better to nibble on you, my dear."

Jordon bent and tenderly captured her lower lip between his teeth.

Gretchen moaned with sweet, unexpected plea-sure. She had been expecting his kiss, not this exquisite assault. Her hands clung to his back as she closed the gap between them. Frustration and desire made her bold. She wanted to taste him. She teasingly ran her tongue over his upper lip.

Jordon released her lower lip and gave her what she wanted. He took her mouth in a kiss that promised wild nights and satisfied mornings. His hands pulled her closer as he leaned against the thick wooden door and allowed her sweetness to wash over him. Desire throbbed and need pounded. He wanted this woman, and he wanted her now. His snow angel was going up in flames in his arms. The mayor of Edelweiss was melting against the man who was going to bring the village into the twentieth century.

Jordon reluctantly broke the kiss and dragged much needed air into his lungs. He couldn't con-tinue to the logical conclusion without Gretchen knowing why he was in Edelweiss.

Gretchen blinked and stepped back a step. Lord, what had happened? She had been kissed by men before, but never with such desired-filled intensity. Dazed and flustered, she tried to act casual. "I don't think that's what happens in the fairy tale."

Three

Gretchen pulled back the cuff of her jacket and glanced at her watch. It was time. Why had she agreed to give Jordon his first ski lesson? Any man who can kiss the way he could didn't need any more lessons in life. He was positively lethal now. If he kissed her on the slopes, she would melt like hot fudge on a sundae and slither her way down to the Dragon's Lair.

She looked around with satisfaction at the distant snow-covered mountains and the village of Edelweiss cradled between Shadow and Donner mountains. From her vantage point Gretchen could pinpoint the lake and locate the speck that was the Dragon's Lair. After spending a sleepless night tossing and turning she had hit the slopes at first light. If common sense wouldn't remove Jordon from her thoughts, maybe physical exhaustion would. Only problem was, she had promised to meet Jordon at the lodge in five minutes.

Sunshine took the bite out of the cold wind that was tossing the thick braid hanging down her back. The sun was brilliant. The weather conditions were perfect for skiing. Gretchen looked up into the blue vastness. Standing at the heart of the White Mountains was as close to heaven a person could get without flying. She knew there were higher mountain ranges throughout the world, but none could equal the beauty that now surrounded her. This was home.

She lowered her goggles, positioned her poles, and pushed off for her last solo run of the day.

Jordon stood outside the lodge watching the skiers. He had arrived fifteen minutes early for his first ski lesson with Gretchen and had walked through the building. She wasn't inside. He was beginning to feel out of place, standing there without any skis, poles, and clunky boots, when he spotted a skier tearing down the mountain. He squinted and held up his hand to shade his eyes.

He frowned as the graceful skier, with a thick blond braid flying, wove her way around other skiers. The red-and-yellow jacket was identical to the one Gretchen wore. As the skier moved closer, he was positive. This was his snow angel.

Gretchen slowed down near the bottom of the mountain. Speed was for the expert trails, not the base of the mountain where beginners and children congregated. The run had left her feeling exhilarated, free, and ready to do it again. Last night when Jordon asked if she were doing anything tomorrow, she had said she was going skiing. Spending the morning teaching a beginner the basics, while she could be flying down the slopes at a higher attitude, wasn't high on her list of exciting things to do. But something had made her agree to meet him.

She didn't know what to do with the man. Logic told her to keep her distance, her heart cried for a chance, and her body shouted, *What are you waiting for?* He had seemed so eager to have her teach him. Gretchen imagined what it would be like being thirty-eight and standing in the beginner's class. She shuddered at the thought.

Her parents had given her her first pair of skis for her third birthday. Everyone expected her to follow in her mother's footsteps, right up to winning an Olympic gold medal in the downhill race. By the time she was sixteen, she was competing, with her sights set on the World Cup. Her life and short career came crashing to a halt the year before she graduated from high school. Her parents had been killed in a tragic skiing accident on Suicide Pass. Gretchen had put away her skis for three years, and with them any chance she might have had for an Olympic gold. Nowadays she skied only for pleasure.

Gretchen headed for the lodge and spotted Jordon immediately. He didn't look too happy. She made a sudden stop, kicking up a small billow of snow less than a foot away from him. She lowered her goggles and grinned. "Glad to see you're on time."

"You were going too fast."

Not sure if she heard him correctly, she asked, "Pardon?"

"I said you were going too fast." At her bewildered look he pointed to the trail she had just descended. "I saw you coming down."

Gretchen glanced at the trail. Only the bottom third of it was visible. The top two thirds were hidden by trees. It was the top portion of the run that kept her enthralled. It was where skill combined with speed that got her adrenaline pumping. It was the part that was in her blood. It was what she was born to do. Even after her parents' death she couldn't bring herself to give up skiing totally. She had stopped the sixty-miles-per-hour downhill plunges and concentrated on having fun. Jordon couldn't have seen how fast she had been going. "I wasn't going too fast, Jordon. The bottom is too crowded to allow for speed."

Jordon yielded. He didn't want to argue with her before his ski lesson even began. Fear had clawed at his stomach when he had realized it was his snow angel barreling down the side of the mountain. She had made it look so smooth and graceful, almost as if she were performing a slow, intimate dance with an imaginary lover. Jordon wanted to be that lover. "So when do I get my skis and make that run with you?"

Gretchen groaned and shook her head. He wanted to run before he could walk. "I'm sorry, Jordon, but that's an advanced trail. If I'm going to teach you, we begin on the beginner's slope or nothing."

He considered his options. Either make a fool out of himself on the kiddie hill or say good-bye to Gretchen's company. "Okay, I'll go give the kids something to laugh at."

She released the bindings on her skis and stepped off. "You won't give the kids anything to laugh at if you don't fall down." She placed her skis and poles in the racks by the doors of the lodge and led the way around the building to the rental shop.

Their first argument came in the rental shop. Jordon wanted regular skis, not the short beginner ones. Gretchen won the argument. Fifteen minutes on the beginner's hill and Jordon's prediction proved correct. Not only had he fallen but he'd managed to take her with him.

For the first time in her life kids were pointing

and laughing at her on skis. Gretchen removed one of his poles from under her bottom, pushed her headband up, and pinned Jordon with an I'm-gonna-kill-you look.

Jordon grinned and wiped a spray of snow off his jaw. "See, I can stop." She looked adorable coated with snowflakes. He reached out and gently removed a glistening flake from the tip of her nose.

Gretchen's resolve melted with his gesture. How could she stay mad when he flashed that dangerous dimple? "I think we need to work on your technique some more."

Laughter danced in his eyes. "No one ever complained about my technique before."

We're not talking about skiing. Her gaze lingered on his mouth. Her voice was soft and wishful as she said, "No, I don't imagine anyone would."

His smile faded, and his new skiing outfit suddenly became too warm. With a quick tug he pulled off a glove and cupped her pink cheek. When he had come to Edelweiss, he hadn't been expecting anything unusual or wonderful to happen. But here she was, sitting in a bed of snow looking like an angel. "Ah, Gretchen, what am I going to do with you?" His thumb tenderly outlined her lower lip. He closed his eyes as memories of last night's kiss flooded his senses.

Kiss me! Gretchen clenched her teeth before the plea tumbled out of her mouth. "You could help me up so that I can demonstrate the snowplow maneuver again."

In a lithe movement Jordon got to his feet and held out his hand for her. He decided not to push the issue of what was happening between them while a group of children were still laughing at them. Besides, they had a lot to discuss before their relationship could progress to the next stage. He was a grown man of thirty-eight, and heated kisses on the front doorstep of the inn wouldn't satisfy his growing appetite for an angel.

Three hours later Gretchen shook the snow off her jacket and hung it in the inn's coat room. She had to admit Jordon was an excellent pupil. He was in superb physical shape and applied logic and reasoning to every aspect of skiing. "You're a fast learner."

Jordon's dimple made a prompt appearance. "Thank you." He hung his jacket next to hers and glanced around the Dragon's Lair's coat room. Now he understood why it was in such disarray. The inn's guests and staff used it to store their ski equipment. "Would you have time tomorrow for another lesson?"

She unsnapped her boots. "Afraid not. The inn is booked solid for the weekend, and the slopes will be crowded. If you're still around on Monday I'd be glad to give you another lesson then."

He leaned against a wall and smiled as she wiggled out of the eye-catching yellow ski pants. "Since you're going to be tied up all weekend, would you join me for dinner this evening?"

Yellow ski pants found another peg. Business was running the Dragon's Lair, pleasure was spending time in Jordon's company. The two had nothing to do with each other. She had come to the conclusion she wanted to get to know Jordon better. His kisses were intoxicating and his manners impeccable. It had been a long time since she had enjoyed the company of a handsome man. "I have a better idea."

Jordon's brow rose in question. Red stretch pants that fitted like second skin outlined her shapely legs from trim ankles to scrumptious thighs. A baggy red-and-white striped sweater blocked the remaining tantalizing view. "What?"

"How about if I cook you dinner?" Sharing dinner with Jordon in a crowded dining room with the staff and other guests watching every move they made sounded like a nightmare.

"Here?" Gretchen spending the evening in the inn's kitchen didn't sound like a better idea to him.

"In my apartment." She slipped her feet into a pair of old loafers.

Confused, he asked, "I thought you lived here."

"I do. I have an apartment on the fourth floor." She headed for the door that led into the inn. "How does seven sound?"

He had thought the day couldn't get any better. It just did. "Fine."

"There's a flight of stairs on the third floor marked 'Private.' Just follow them up." She opened the door. "I have some business to take care of this afternoon. I'll see you then."

Jordon watched her walk away and grinned. Little Red Riding Hood had just invited the big bad wolf into her home.

Gretchen glanced at the clock on the microwave as the knock sounded on her door. Jordon was one minute early. A soft smile curved her lips as she opened the door. The sight of a dozen red roses surprised her.

"Good evening." Jordon handed her the flowers. "These are for you."

She backed into the apartment and shook her head. The man was impossible. "Hi."

Jordon glanced curiously around the room. He

believed you could tell a lot about people by their homes. "Is red your favorite color?"

Gretchen chuckled and delicately sniffed the lovely blooms. "No. Are you planning on sending me flowers in every color under the rainbow until you guess it?"

He frowned at the living room. It was a contradiction in tastes. Thick, sturdy wood furniture that looked as if it originally came from the Alps was mixed with some pieces of early-American and Eastern design. "Could I buy a flower in your favorite color?"

"Most definitely." She took a final sniff. "Thank you, Jordon, they're lovely."

Double glass doors that led to a snow-packed balcony took up the far wall. A low white couch holding dozens of pillows in every color imaginable was placed in front of a fireplace. A hand-hewn cupboard painted in the customary bright colors of traditional folk art captured his eye. It shouted "family heirloom" and "expensive." A stark white area rug covered most of the pine floor, and the walls and ceiling were painted white. White was the dominant color, but the room wasn't colorless or drab by any means. He noticed the yellow roses, from yesterday, sitting on the coffee table.

He turned to ask what the delicious smell was, when a glimmer of light caught his attention. A two-foot-high purple dragon was in a corner, seemingly guarding the door. Astonished that he hadn't noticed it right away, he walked over to it. "The dragon in the Dragon's Lair?"

Gretchen opened a kitchen cabinet and searched for another vase. "No. My apartment is off-limits to guests. If you look around, you'll find quite a few of the beasts throughout it." She opened another cabinet. "Make yourself at home while I put these in water."

Jordon ran his finger over the purple crystals that were the dragon's eyes. He was a majestic creature covered in purple scales and teal-colored armor breastplates. He looked ferocious, wise, and vulnerable. As if he knew he was the last of his species and that with him rested the last hope of all dragonkind.

"I have to step next door to get a vase. I'll be right back."

"Next door?"

"The supply room for the inn is on this floor. There's a door connecting my apartment to it." She started to walk down the hall with Jordon following. "Would you like to see it?"

"Sure." He could have added that anything she did fascinated him. When she flipped on the lights, he saw shelves and boxes overflowing the room. "There's a lot of stuff in here."

Without missing a beat, she located a crystal vase on a shelf. "If you think this is crowded, you should see a supply room for a major hotel. The Dragon's Lair has only twenty-four guest rooms."

He spotted sliding metal double doors. "There's an elevator."

"Of course. How did you think we got all this stuff up here?" She glanced fondly at the piles of linen, boxes of dishes, and odd pieces of furniture cluttering the room. This room was as much a part of her as her skis. Not wanting Jordon to become bored, she headed back toward the apartment. "We'd better be going." She turned off the light and shut the door. "I have a confession to make."

"Oh?"

"I didn't cook the dinner we're about to have."

She shrugged her shoulders and handed Jordon two empty plates and pointed to the table. "I ran into some problems that needed my attention, and before I knew it, it was six-thirty."

Jordon glanced down at the plates and bit back a chuckle. He was required to help set the table. He couldn't remember the last time a female had invited him to dinner and then expected him to pitch in and help. Most women tended to fuss over him. He positioned the plates closer than necessary on the table. The one woman he wouldn't mind fussing over him had delegated him to be kitchen helper. "We could have gone out for dinner."

"The Dragon's Lair has the best restaurant in Edelweiss." She handed him the cutlery and went back into the kitchen. "I hope you like chicken."

"What, no sausage or fondue?"

Gretchen laughed as she carried over a tray laden with food brought up from the inn's kitchen. "We're trying to offer a healthier choice for our guests."

He helped her finish setting the table and politely held out the chair for her. "Everything looks delicious."

She glanced at the wonderful assortment of food. "To think all it took was a frantic phone call to Effie in the kitchen twenty minutes ago."

He liked her honesty. "I'm sure you would have done as fine a job if time had permitted."

A tint of pink colored her cheeks. "I did manage to make the coffee."

Jordon dug into his dinner. Skiing built an appetite, he'd discovered. After he had left Gretchen in the lobby, he had ordered a sandwich and a pot of coffee from room service, then spent the afternoon going over mounds of compiled data. Edelweiss was the perfect village for his condominiums. Not only would it help the local economy but his own company would stand to make a substantial profit. All he needed to do was to convince Gretchen and the town council.

Now, as he sat beside her on the couch, he wondered how to bring up the subject. They had cleaned the table and loaded the dishwasher. He had never known how intimate the small confines of a kitchen could be. The sweet floral scent of Gretchen's perfume had tempted his senses as they had both bent to place a glass in the dishwasher. Her light laughter had floated above the running water as she rinsed off a plate, and captured his attention. He had breathed a sigh of relief when they left the kitchen and brought their dessert and coffee into the living room.

"Would you like me to light the fire?"

Jordon put his cup down. "I could do that."

"That's okay. It's all ready to go, all it needs is a match." She bent and touched off the kindling with a flick of a match.

He watched as light from the flames reflected off her outfit. A loose-fitting teal-colored silk blouse was tucked into a baggy pair of pants made out of the same material. A silver belt was wrapped around her slim waist, and a pair of silver slippers glimmered on her feet. Fancy silver barrettes kept her long hair streaming down her back and out of her face. Gretchen looked like an exotic jewel.

Gretchen returned to the couch and picked up her dessert. This was the part of dating that she hated. The can-we-find-something-in-common-to-talk-about stage. The majority of men she had dated failed it. They were either too preoccupied with making fast moves or so full of themselves that she was always amazed their heads didn't swell right there and then. Spending hours in a man's company listening to him boast about his job, income, or his new sports car rated right up there with stripping the wax off the kitchen floor.

She curled her feet up under her and relaxed against the pillows. "So, you enjoyed skiing enough to try it again."

"I had an excellent teacher." He took a sip of coffee. "Do you think there's room to expand the ski area?"

"Why, wasn't it big enough for you?" Gretchen chuckled.

"Sure it was. But you said it was going to get crowded this weekend."

"Every ski area in New England draws a crowd on the weekends. Shadow and Thunder mountains will get their share."

"What happens if Edelweiss grows? Won't the ski area have to be expanded?"

"Edelweiss isn't growing." Gretchen frowned, and set her uneaten strudel on the coffee table.

"But say it does?"

"It won't."

"Why?" He sat his empty cup next to his untouched dessert.

"Listen, Jordon, I don't expect someone from New York to understand the delicate balance Edelweiss is trying to achieve."

"How did you know I was from New York?"

Gretchen forced herself to meet his gaze and hold it. "I checked with the registration desk." *There, I admitted to being interested.*

A slow, knowing smile curved his mouth. "What delicate balance are you referring to?"

He knows I'm interested, so why are we talking about Edelweiss? "We're trying to offer a glimpse of some Swiss traditions to our guests and still have the comfortable feel of America. To many this is as close to Switzerland as they will ever get, while others come for the uniqueness. Edelweiss is a charming, safe, and secure village in a world that sometimes goes quite insane. We offer a glimpse into another way of life. We strive for a relaxed, informal, good-time atmosphere."

"You sound like a travel brochure."

Her nose rose an inch. "I am the mayor, you know."

Jordon chuckled and lightly tapped the tip of her nose. "You don't kiss like any mayor I know."

Drawn by the laughter sparkling in his eyes, she asked, "How many mayors have you kissed?"

"One." The back of his fingers lightly brushed the delicate skin of her neck. "She is this incredibly sexy mayor of some Swiss village named Liverwurst or something."

A trail of heat followed his fingers to the collar of her blouse. "Where did you come up with that name?"

Jordon cradled her neck with his palm and tilted her face with his thumb. "My mind went blank. The only German I could think of was the punchline from one of Hans's jokes." His breath feathered across her waiting lips.

Gretchen ran her tongue over her lower lip in anticipation. She didn't have to wait long. Jordon lowered his mouth the fraction of an inch she needed to savor the moistness of his mouth.

His gentle siege lasted only an instant before he pulled back and smiled. "I think you ought to run for governor."

She tried to hide her disappointment at his withdrawal. "Why not president?"

He kissed her pout and sat back. "Too many security people." Needing something to do with his hands before he reached for her again, he picked up his plate of strudel. "What would happen if more people moved to Edelweiss?"

Gretchen didn't want to talk about Edelweiss. In fact she didn't want to talk at all. "People won't move here."

"Why not? It seems like the perfect place to live or to build a vacation home."

"People have to have jobs to support themselves. Edelweiss can barely support its residents now, never mind their children. What will all these fine people be doing in Edelweiss?"

"Shopping in your businesses, building the economy, and trying to hobknob with the rich."

Gretchen laughed. "Jordon, in case you haven't noticed, we have no celebrities."

He raised his fork and punctuated the air. It was time for Gretchen to see the future and the glory it can behold. "But you will."

She shivered as a chill slid down her spine. Uneasiness caused her voice to tremble as she asked, "How?"

Breaking the number-one rule in his business, he allowed his personal feelings to override his common sense. "Because I will be building a fifty-unit condominium complex at the base of Shadow Mountain."

Gretchen stared horrified as Jordon flashed his dimpled grin. The big bad wolf was showing his teeth, and what he wanted to eat was Edelweiss.

Four

She quickly jumped to her feet and nearly knocked over the coffee table. Her voice quivered with rage. "Over my dead body you will."

Jordon's grin slowly faded as he cautiously set down his plate. "Now, Gretchen—"

"Don't you 'now, Gretchen' me, you . . . you . . . you . . . shyster." The last word came out sounding like it was a disease a person would get from living under a rock.

"Shyster!" Jordon echoed as he leaped to his feet and stood toe-to-toe with Gretchen. After all the agonizing and debating he had done with himself over telling her about the condos, she had the audacity to call him names. He was unable to think of an appropriate response, and his voice trembled with fury as he repeated the offensive label, "Shyster!"

Her hand indicated the yellow roses. "Is that was this has been all about?"

"What?"

"Dazzle the gullible mayor with flowers and

delicious kisses and she'll let you build your stupid condominiums?"

Jordon's fingers clenched into tight fists. His back was ramrod straight as he glared down his nose. "I have *never* tried to bribe an official in my life. Let alone use flowers and delicious kisses, as you so politely put it."

Gretchen took a hesitant step backward. Did she somehow misinterpret his actions? "Are you by chance talking about the Beckers' place?"

"I'm referring to one hundred and sixty-two prime acres that my company has an option on."

Gretchen paled. It was too late if his company already held the option. Her shoulders slumped in defeat as she turned and walked over to the glass doors. In the pale moonlight she could see the dark, hulking mass of Shadow Mountain. His modern condominiums would be visible from the living-room balcony. The other balcony, off her bedroom, faced Thunder Mountain. She raised her trembling hand and pressed it against the cool glass.

It was happening again. Was there an invisible sign around her neck that only unscrupulous males could see that read CAN BE BOUGHT WITH A LITTLE ROMANCE? She thought she had learned her lesson five years ago with Tom. At least this time things hadn't gone that far. She stared at Jordon's reflection in the glass. Tom had been pretty-boy handsome, whereas Jordon was arresting in his masculinity. Tom had used her position at the top to boost his way up the corporate ladder. She had never granted Tom special privileges or promotions while being his lover, but other officials did. She had blindly fallen for Tom's flowery speeches of love-ever-after. Until that fatal night fives years ago when she caught him going through her private files and using the privileged information for his own gain. Her dreams were smashed and the trust she had always held in people shattered, she came home to Edelweiss to heal.

Gretchen noticed that Jordon hadn't moved. He was silently waiting. This time she wasn't going to run. Her heart was still safe. Not turning around to face him, she said in a calm and strong voice, "You would have to get the town council's and my approval before you could build on the property."

"I know."

His stance seemed to relax somewhat. Maybe he didn't understand. "Edelweiss has some of the toughest building ordinances in the state."

"So I've read."

Gretchen's eyes squinted at the glass. "Are these units you're planning to build Swiss in design?"

His answer came plain and simple. "No."

She turned around at his reply. He was perfectly serious. The man had come to Edelweiss knowing the rules and was blatantly trying to ignore them. "I'm sorry, Jordon, but there is no way we will allow you to build fifty modern condominiums on that piece of property."

A small smile touched the corner of his mouth. The mayor was now speaking, not his Gretchen. Surprised at the thought, he wondered when she had become *his* Gretchen. He liked the way it sounded. "Don't you want to wait until you have all the facts?"

She had noticed his satisfied smile. "No." Pleased by his sudden frown, she put on her most gracious hostess smile. "My, look at the time. I didn't realize it was that late."

Jordon knew a hint when it slapped him in the

face. He refused to take the bait. "It's only eight-thirty. The night is still young."

It was Gretchen's turn to frown. If the man couldn't take a hint, she'd have to be blunt. "I really think it's about time you left."

Jordon's dimple flashed. His Gretchen was back. He calmly sat down and picked up his dessert. "I haven't eaten my strudel yet."

She had to get him out of her apartment fast. She didn't like the way her stomach turned all hot and mushy when he flashed that dimple. It spelled trouble. Especially now that she knew why he was in Edelweiss. Being made a fool of once could be chalked up to innocence, but twice would be the result of stupidity. She was many things; stupid wasn't one of them. Her voice held a note of desperation. "Take your dessert with you." Who cared that it was sitting on the china her great-grandmother had lovingly wrapped and carried to America. Sacrifices had to be made. Better one plate than her heart.

Jordon chuckled and picked up his fork. "Wouldn't dream of it." Seeing her confused expression, he held up his empty cup. "Do you have any more of that delicious coffee?"

Gretchen bit her lip and ran through her options. She could physically throw him out. Considering his size, she would have to call for Gunter to help, which would raise more than a few eyebrows. Or she could feed the jerk and pray that he didn't flash any more dimples before he left. He had made a very huge mistake by telling her his intentions. She now knew where he was coming from. She also knew where he was going— nowhere. She took the cup from him and silently headed into the kitchen. The faster he got his coffee, the faster he would be leaving.

Jordon realized something very important as he watched her stalk away. Gretchen didn't want to call attention to the fact she was entertaining a guest in her private quarters by raising a fuss and throwing him out. Was it because he was a guest or because he was male? He turned and stared at the bouquet of yellow roses. One thing was certain—before he left tonight, he would clear up any misunderstanding about the flowers.

Gretchen returned with his coffee and another cup for herself. She sat down on the only chair in the room. The couch seemed too intimate. Too close to temptation. How could she be mad enough to throttle him and still be tempted to run her fingers through his hair? The man was dangerous.

He glanced at the silent woman sitting by the fire and noticed the slight trembling in her fingers as she clutched her coffee. She was still upset about the condominiums. Well, hell, he was still upset about being called a shyster. A soft smile touched his lips as he wondered if any of his employees had ever been called a shyster while out trying to move their stumbling blocks. He'd bet this year's Christmas bonus none of them ever had. The gentle firelight highlighted Gretchen's golden hair and illuminated the silky sheen of moisture on her mouth. Thoughts of trying to move this particular obstacle sent a shaft of uneasiness into his gut. He wanted to comfort her, not overpower her. Either the stumbling blocks were getting higher or he was going soft.

"Firelight suits you." She raised her eyes at the sound of his voice. He saw anger blend with vulnerability in their blue depths. Understanding dawned. "Who was he?"

"Who?"

He carefully placed the fragile plate on the table. "The man who made you doubt?"

Gretchen crossed her legs and nervously tapped the side of her mug with her pink-tipped finger-nails. "I don't know what you're talking about."

Jordon rose and slowly walked toward her. "Yes, you do." He took the cup out of her hands and sat it on the end table. "Somebody hurt you, and I want to know who."

Her chin rose in stubbornness. Jordon might be intimidating as all hell standing over her, but this was her home. "Are you referring to the other *shyster* who tried to buy me with pretty flowers and kisses?"

Jordon's eyes narrowed at the last word. The mere thought of another man kissing her sent a wave of violence pulsating through his veins. He could forgive the name-calling, for the time being, but he would never forget the vision of her in another man's arms. "If I wanted to buy you, it wouldn't be with flowers. I'd come right out and name a figure too good to pass up."

She sniffed at his audacity.

He tenderly cupped her chin and forced her gaze to lock with his. "The flowers were for Gretchen Horst, the woman, not Gretchen Horst, the mayor of Edelweiss."

Unable to resist, she asked, "And the kisses?"

The dimple appeared with his wolfish grin. "The kisses were for me." He brushed her lips with his own. "All for me." He covered her purr of delight with his mouth and tasted heaven.

Gretchen raised her hands, unsure if she was pulling him closer or pushing him away. Common sense said to push him away; the delicious desires coursing through her body were screaming for more. Her fingers tangled in his silken hair, and a groan sounded deep in her throat as his tongue swept past her lips. She felt herself standing and melting into his arms.

Jordon wrapped his arms around her and pulled her closer. The full softness of her breasts pressed into his chest. Hot need pulsed through every fiber of his being. He wanted this woman. The coolness of her smooth blouse turned to silken fire beneath his hand. His hands slid lower and pulled the sweet curve of her hips against his hardening body.

Gretchen felt the rigid evidence of his arousal pressing against her and came crashing back to earth. Her eyes opened wide as she broke the kiss and took a dazed step backward.

Jordon released his hold and let her go as he dragged much-needed air into his lungs. Talk about having the wind knocked out of you. Hell, when Gretchen responded so sweetly to his kisses, he felt as if a tornado were ripping through his body.

Gretchen could see his stunned expression. Well, it couldn't be any worse than hers. Not only had she allowed him to kiss her, she had responded! In another minute she would probably have been ripping off his clothes.

A tender smile teased the corner of his mouth. She looked more shocked than he felt. His thumb was gentle as he brushed her swollen, moist lower lip. "You should come with a warning label from the surgeon general."

Gretchen closed her eyes and tried to will the sensations flooding her body to leave. They didn't obey.

His voice was low and rough as he said, "Warning: Kissing may be hazardous to your health." He gently cupped her flushed cheek. "If I had a heart problem, I'd be a dead man right about now."

Gretchen forced herself to take another step backward. *And if you hadn't told me about the condos, we would have been in bed right this minute.* She flinched as the truth hit her. As much as she loathed what Jordon wanted to do, she was still attracted to him. "I think it's about time you left."

Jordon jammed his hands into his trousers pockets before he could do something stupid. Like shake her until she saw reason. What they had just shared had nothing to do with building ordinances or Edelweiss. It had been between one particular man and one particular woman. No other two people on earth could duplicate that feeling. The intense need had knocked him for a loop and sent a flash of fear dancing along his spine. The control he had always prided himself on having over his life had swiftly disappeared as he held Gretchen in his arms. He was unsure how to regain that control. But one thing was for sure—leaving before he had a chance to set Gretchen straight would be a big mistake. He ran his fingers through his hair and retreated back to the couch. "I think we need to talk."

"I really don't think we have anything to talk about."

He cocked an eyebrow. "Sit down, Gretchen, before I come back over there, and then we won't be *talking.*"

Gretchen understood what he was referring to and sat. Sometimes compliance was the best policy. Feeling brave with half a room between them, she said, "So talk."

Jordon took a ragged breath and rested his

elbows on his knees. She was pushing him. "Have you always been a coward?"

Gretchen leaped to her feet. "Coward!" Fury colored her face.

"Sit back down," he said. "My control is dangling by a thread as it is."

Her eyes widened in fear.

"Dammit, Gretchen. I'm not going to hurt you. If you continue to prance that sexy bottom in front of me, we are going to end up in bed, and then we won't have this discussion till morning."

A red haze danced in front of her eyes. That did it! The man was out of here. She stormed across the room. He was going to leave if she had to pick him up bodily and throw him down the stairs. Her hand was on the knob ready to fling open the door when his palm flattened against it. Her gaze could have seared his hand. "Move it or lose it."

"I didn't mean it the way it sounded." He glanced at her determined profile and groaned. "Hell, maybe I did. I don't know anymore." He kept his hand on the door and backed off as far as possible. He didn't want to scare her. "You have me so tied up in knots that I don't know if I'm coming or going."

"Going." She turned to face him. "Definitely going."

Jordon sighed. If he were this clumsy with his tongue in the boardroom, his business would have had to file for Chapter Thirteen years ago. "Could we sit back down and try this again?" Noticing her obstinate stare, he added, "Please." Her expression relaxed only slightly. He tried his most charming smile. "I'm sorry for calling you a coward." He waited for her to retract the shyster slur.

He waited in vain. She gave a slight nod of her

head and led the way back to the kitchen table. After flicking a switch and flooding the room with light she sat down. As long as he was apologizing, she might as well listen to what he had to say. Being the mayor, she had a responsibility to Edelweiss. She glanced up and politely smiled at his exasperated expression. "You wanted to talk?"

Jordon bit back a curse and matched her plastic smile. His Gretchen was proving to have a stiffer backbone than he was accustomed to. He sat down in the chair opposite her and wondered exactly who was calling all the shots. "When I accepted your invitation to dinner, I did so as Jordon Winters, the man, not as president of Winters Enterprises. The flowers were sent because you're a very attractive, intelligent woman, whom I find extremely sexy."

Gretchen prayed the pleasure his words caused didn't show in her expression.

Jordon noticed the faint flush and took heart. "I didn't know you were the mayor until dinner the first night when Hans interrupted our dessert."

"Then you quickly settled the bill and disappeared." She remembered her disappointment of his sudden departure. "The flowers arrived the next afternoon. What did you do, go back to your room and plan your strategy?" She smiled in satisfaction at exposing his plan. "You should have tried chocolates. They're my weakness."

"I'll remember that for the future," Jordon growled. His fingers drummed on the tabletop as he studied her gleeful expression. The woman didn't know her own worth. She honestly thought he was interested in her only because she was the mayor. Some bastard must have done a really good job on her. "He must have really hurt you."

Gretchen's smile faded. "Who?"

"The man who taught you to doubt yourself." He ignored her stricken expression. "I refuse to suffer for another man's sins, Gretchen."

"Are you that sure it was a man?"

Her question proved he was on the right track. "A woman wouldn't have made you doubt your own femininity." She realized too late that she had just admitted he was correct. "Don't worry, Gretchen. I'm going to prove you're wrong."

"How do you propose to do that?"

"Not only am I going to build those condominiums, but I will continue to want you far after the ink is dry on those contracts."

One brow rose at his arrogance. "Be still, my beating heart." She lightly tapped her chest and fluttered her eyelashes. "I do declare, Mr. Winters, you leave me breathless with your pretty speeches."

Jordon chuckled. "I'd be the first to admit that rated a zero as far as romantic statements go. But it is the truth. I want you more than any other woman I've ever met, and the condominiums be damned."

Gretchen swallowed the anxiety clawing at her throat. He meant every word he was saying. She could see it in his eyes. "But will you still want me if the deal falls through?"

Jordon heard the vulnerability in her voice and slammed his fist against the table in frustration. "I want that bastard's name."

She flinched and slowly shook her head. If she gave him Tom's name, she could be charged with being an accessory to murder; he looked mad enough to strangle someone.

"Are you still in love with him?"

"Good Lord, no!" Gretchen shrieked.

Seeing her appalled expression, Jordon relaxed. "That might save his life." After a moment, he asked, "Does he live in Edelweiss?" He wasn't sure he could resist the temptation if he happened to bump into the scoundrel on the street.

"No, you're three thousand miles off." She straightened her back and forced the tension in her hands to ease. "Besides, it's ancient history."

"History that you're afraid will repeat itself."

"That's the funny thing about history. If you don't learn anything from it the first time, it undoubtedly will repeat itself."

Jordon mulled over her comment. "Okay, I can see where you might exercise a little bit of caution. But I have two questions for you."

"Only two?"

"Why would I spend all my time and energy bribing only the mayor when it also takes the entire six-man town council's vote to change the building ordinance?" He watched as she chewed her lower lip. "All my reports indicate that you aren't married or involved with any member of the council."

"Of course I'm not. They're all happily married men."

"So there's no reason for me to think you can influence these gentlemen."

"Of course not! When my opinion is asked for, I give it. The council is made up of six different individuals, who are perfectly capable of making a decision on their own. That's why we have a town council—so one person can't control the entire town."

"Aha!" Jordon grinned. "Then why would I single you out?"

Gretchen frowned. There had to be a loophole in his reasoning somewhere, but she couldn't find it yet.

"My second question is more important. And

this one I expect an answer to." He waited until he had her complete attention. "When you kissed that jerk, did it feel the same as when you kissed me?"

She stared into the depths of his gray eyes as he patiently waited for his answer. How could she possibly compare the two? Tom's kisses had been pleasant, warm, and comfortable. Desire curled in her abdomen as she remembered the kisses she had shared with Jordon. They had been exciting, hot, and arousing. She had never known that the simple act of kissing could be so stimulating. Since Jordon had been honest enough to bring up his company's plans before she made a complete fool out of herself by ripping off his clothes, Gretchen took the first hesitant step toward believing him. She gave an honest answer in return. "No, Jordon, there is no comparison."

Every ounce of Jordon's energy was focused on not jumping out of the chair and pulling her into his arms. He wanted to kiss her. He wanted to shout for joy. He wanted to lay her down on satin sheets and erase the memory of every other man from her mind.

Jordon did none of those things. He sat there with a grin plastered across his face and said, "Thank you."

Gretchen shifted nervously in her seat. Misgivings assaulted her mind. Had she just committed a grievous error? She glanced at Jordon and knew her life had just taken a major turn down the mountain of life. She was unsure if the trail she had chosen was going to be smooth sailing or a suicide pass.

Jordon read her doubts and backed off. "Now it really is getting late." He stood up and glanced into the living room. He never got to eat his dessert. "Walk me to the door."

Gretchen hid her confusion as she stood. He was leaving without venturing in the door to her heart that she had cracked open. Her feet didn't make a sound as she softly padded across the floor. She was deciding if she should bring up his next skiing lesson when his voice pulled her from her thoughts.

"Thank you for dinner, Gretchen. It was delicious." He cupped her cheek. "I know this is going to get awfully confusing, and I'm sorry for that, but my hands are tied. The option on the land went into effect six days ago, and my company will lose a hefty sum of money if I back out now."

She was afraid she already knew the answer, but she asked the question anyway. "Have you ever backed out of a business deal?"

He frowned as his thumb outlined the curve of her cheekbone. "No." Her lips parted in a silent invitation. "Have you ever considered resigning from being the mayor?"

Her breath caught as he gazed at her mouth. "No."

"Lord, if I had known mayors looked like you, I would have gone into politics instead of construction."

She blushed and leaned against the door for support. Her knees were turning into mush.

"I'm going to have to talk to the mayor of Edelweiss sooner or later concerning the condos." Regret deepened his voice.

"I know."

"When I do, you will definitely know it's a business meeting."

Her fingers itched to feel the rough texture of his jaw. "How?"

Jordon gave a rueful smile. "Hopefully I won't be staring at your mouth as if it contained the gift of life." He tenderly traced the seductive fullness of her lower lip and shivered as his finger grazed the bottom row of even white teeth. "I'd be cool-headed and rational." His light chuckle indicated he was anything but that now. "And I'm really praying that I would have enough self-control not to walk into any business meeting with you aroused."

Gretchen's boldness surprised even her as she lightly nipped at his finger. His heated moan brought a fresh blush to her highly flushed face. The man was absolutely dangerous. She should be ushering him out the door with instructions to call her in the morning and set up an appointment to see the mayor. The man could be setting her up for the biggest fall of her life, but right this minute she didn't care. She needed to believe in him.

His gaze never leaving her mouth, he asked, "May I kiss you good night?"

Her answer went unheard, but he read the word that formed on her perfectly shaped mouth: *Please.*

He meant the kiss to be short and sweet. But his noble intentions went on a sabbatical the instant he felt her lips part, giving him access to the territory beyond.

Gretchen stood on her tiptoes and met him halfway. Her tongue initiated the erotic dance, her fingers gloried in the slightly rough texture of his cheek, and her breasts swelled with the need to be touched. Her back pressed against the door as he deepened the kiss to this side of sinful.

Jordon forced his hands to press into the door and not touch the soft, yielding woman glued to the front of him. If he touched her, he would lose what little control was left. The mere feel of her breasts cushioning his chest and the knowledge that her hips were tilted upward to press against his throbbing arousal was enough to send him over the edge. Underneath all her fiery passion beat the heart of a cautious woman. If he allowed the passion to win tonight, she would wake to the morning light with nothing but doubts.

He wanted the passion, but he wanted her heart more. He could wait.

Jordon eased up on the kiss until it ended in soft, playful nips. He smiled at the confused emotions clouding her usually blue eyes. "The hardest thing I will ever do in my life is to walk out this door."

She wanted to tell him to stay. She wanted to tell him to leave. He had her so confused, she didn't know what she wanted anymore.

"One night I won't walk out this door, but it won't be tonight. When that night happens, you will want it not only with your body but with your heart." He tenderly placed a light kiss on her moist, swollen mouth.

Gretchen didn't doubt him for a moment. What they had just shared far surpassed any threat of modern glass-and-steel condominiums. With the warmth his statement generated still short-circuiting her common sense, she asked, "Would you like to go ice-skating tomorrow night?"

"Ice-skating?" He had been hoping for another dinner invitation.

"Every Friday night there's an ice-skating party at the pond."

He saw her hopeful look. "I've never ice-skated before, but I'm willing to give it a try."

A radiant smile lit her face as he opened the door and stepped out onto the landing. "I'll meet you in the lobby around nine."

He brushed a soft kiss across her tempting mouth. He would have rather met her at this particular door, but he didn't push the issue. He would allow her to set the pace. For the time being. "Sweet dreams."

Gretchen leaned against the doorjamb with a grin spread across her face and watched as he disappeared down the flight of steps.

Five

Gretchen fidgeted with the prim white collar of her blouse and nervously straightened the lapels on the navy blazer. The suit was the most business-like outfit in her closet. It was perfect for the up-coming appointment between a Mr. Jordon Winters of Winters Enterprises and the mayor of Edelweiss.

Jordon's voice had sounded so cool and profes-sional hours earlier when he had called and set up the meeting for this afternoon. She had no trouble figuring out that this meeting was to be strictly business. She glanced around her small, clut-tered office off the reception area of the Dragon's Lair and frowned. It didn't project a very business-like atmosphere, but it was the best she could do. The mayor of Edelweiss had no official office, and the town council held their monthly meetings in the banquet hall of the firehouse. When she was required to hold a small meeting, she usually did it in her apartment. The thought of conducting business with Jordon over her kitchen table left a bad taste in her mouth. Hence the twelve-by-twelve office jammed into an eight-by-six area.

She picked up a stack of books from a chair and jerked around as a loud knock sounded on the door.

Jordon entered Gretchen's office and quickly ran his assessing gaze over her. Her hair was pulled back into a prim bun, and dainty pearl studs adorned her ears. A lifeless blue suit concealed all her luscious curves, and the high-necked blouse seemed to be choking her. She looked like a nun on vacation. Good! He just might make it through this meeting without embarrassing himself. "Good afternoon, Ms. Horst." He held out his hand. "Thank you for taking the time to see me."

Gretchen stared at his outstretched hand and gulped. She wasn't sure this was such a good idea. There was no way she could calmly shake his hand and not remember the erotic dream that had plagued her sleep last night. She barely touched his fingertips before retreating behind her desk. "I believe you mentioned something about the possibilities of your company building condominiums."

Jordon's smile was pure business as he nonchalantly placed his briefcase on the already crowded desk and flipped the latches.

Gretchen stared at the mound of paperwork in front of her and sighed. Had she really promised Jordon that she would read everything and get back to him soon? The man had to be part magician with a slice of a hypnotist thrown in for good measure. They had sat crowded together in this small office and discussed business for over an hour. Really discussed business! The man was phenomenal. He had done his homework on Edelweiss, the surrounding area, and the general condition of the entire East Coast. For every one of her questions he had an answer, or he quickly scribbled her concern on a thick yellow legal pad. For every one of her protests he countered with an equally strong argument. Jordon Winters was definitely a force to be reckoned with when he wanted something.

She lifted several sheets and frowned. How in the hell had Jordon gotten his hands on an impact study of Edelweiss?

Two hours later as the light started to fade outside the only window in the room she wearily shifted her shoulders and lowered the report she had been reading. A person could die of eyestrain trying to build condominiums. No wonder Jordon had to put on glasses to figure out which report was in his hand. He had looked so professional in his dark-gray suit, conservative red tie, and thick glasses. Nothing like the lover from her dreams last night.

Gretchen slowly rose from the chair and stretched. The dining room would be opening its doors soon. She had to get ready to greet the new influx of guests that had been arriving since noon. Weekends in the dead of winter leaned toward the chaotic side. Everyone wanted to jam as much as possible into their forty-eight hours of fun. The toll was taken by Gretchen and her loyal staff.

She left the mound of reports scattered across her desk and shut off the light. Time enough later to finish reading the stack of papers. With a weary sigh she closed the door and headed for her apartment. Nothing had changed. Her mind was still made up. Contemporary condominiums would dot Edelweiss's skyline when Shadow and Thunder mountains crumbled with age, and not a millennium sooner.

Her hand froze on the silken cord strung across the bottom of her private steps to the apartment. A small pot of pale-purple violets sat on each step. She picked up the first plant and reconnected the cord behind her. Three trips and fourteen pots later she sat stunned on her couch. Her coffee table was overflowing with dainty lavender blooms and furry green leaves. Matching satin lavender ribbons decorated each plant. She picked up the card that had been sticking out of the plant on the top step. *Is it lavender? Looking forward to nine o'clock. "J."* He was going to do it! He was going to send her flowers in every color until he guessed. Maybe she should tell him what her favorite color was and put an end to this extravagance. With a tender touch she gently ran her finger over a thick leaf and softly smiled as it tickled her. The leaf felt hairy. Dare she keep all fourteen plants? How in the world was she going to keep them alive? Gunter paled every time she walked across the Dragon's Lair's lawn. Grass had been known to die from her mere footfall, and trees shuddered as she passed beneath them. Her green thumb was as brown as dirt.

Gretchen glanced at her watch and jumped to her feet. She was going to be late, and all because she had been daydreaming over a bunch of flowers that weren't even her favorite color. She was halfway across the room heading for the shower when she stopped and turned around. Fourteen fragile plants seem to be pleading for her attention. Recalling her grandmother's words that all a plant needed was dirt, sunshine, water, and love she bit her lip. They already had the dirt, and sunshine would have to wait until morning. With hurried footsteps she raced to the kitchen and filled a pitcher with water. Her voice was low and sweet as she sang a lullaby in German to the plants and great quantities of water doused their already-moist soil.

Jordon moved away from the wall as Gretchen breezed into the lobby. She was five minutes late. He grinned as she tried to steady her breathing. She was either very excited to see him or, more than likely, just ran down the three flights of stairs. "Are you that anxious to see me?"

She shifted her skates over her shoulder, grabbed his hand, and pulled him into the mudroom. "We have to hurry." If it wasn't for his dumb plants dripping water all over her white living-room rug she would have been on time.

He was still pulling on his jacket wondering what was going on when she shoved him out the back door. A sleigh full of people stood waiting.

Gunter held Zelda's reins as the horse's misty breath clouded the cold night air. He handed the leather straps to Gretchen as she climbed up onto the driver's seat. "'Bout time you got here," he grumbled.

Gretchen flashed a fetching grin over her shoulder to the eight passengers snuggled under colorful lap blankets. "Sorry about being a few minutes late. An emergency came up." She felt Jordon join her on the small wooden bench. "Everyone ready?"

A chorus of fun-filled cheers spilled into the night. With a light flick of her wrist she set Zelda into a brisk trot. The metallic peal of Zelda's bells filled the air.

Jordon moved closer to Gretchen. She was wearing the red cape, leather gloves, and a pair of black boots. She looked adorable and kissable. He glared at the passengers. Their first sleigh ride he had had her all to himself. "This almost has a familiar feeling to it."

"Stop scowling at the guests, Jordon." Her light musical voice softened the reprimand.

His whisper was low and rough. "I've been dying to kiss you since you walked into the dining room hours ago looking gorgeous and sexy."

She almost dropped the reins. It was on the tip of her tongue to ask why he didn't, when the boisterous laughter of the guests registered in her passion-filled mind. So much for privacy. Wasn't that why she invited him to come skating? so that she could spend some time with him and not be alone? Jordon Winters alone was just too tempting.

In the pale moonlight reflecting off the white, glistening snow, he observed her trepidation. She was just as aware of him as he was of her. The kiss he wanted became an obsession.

This afternoon's business meeting was a farce. He had walked into her office intending to be professional and had left throbbing and aching. His suit jacket had hidden the evidence of his lack of self-control. Ten minutes in a freezing-cold shower had only appeased the torment. When she drifted around the dining room seeing to her guests' comfort, the ache had returned. He had to force himself to remain in his seat and finish his dinner instead of throwing the provocative innkeeper over his shoulder and carrying her to his room. The meeting had shown him that Gretchen was a worthy "stumbling block," one that he would do well in remembering not to underestimate.

He slid a glance at the laughing, carefree passengers. They all appeared young, healthy, and ready to have a ball. Gretchen was laughing at something one of the women in the back had shouted. Could everyone be this enthusiastic about spending a couple of hours on thin metal blades gliding across hard ice covering a deep body of water, or had they spent the last hour in the lounge fortifying themselves?

The sounds of shouts and laughter reached them before they spotted the pond. Jordon could see the distant glow of bonfires filtering through the trees.

"We're almost there," Gretchen shouted. Zelda quickened her trot down the path she had been traveling for the past two years. A warm shelter and a tasty carrot were always waiting at its end.

Curious, Jordon craned his neck for his first glimpse of the pond and paled. It wasn't some cute little pond that, if he fell through it, would get his knees wet. "That's not a pond!"

Gretchen loosened her grip on the reins and allowed Zelda the freedom to finish the journey. "Of course not. That's Lake Conquest."

"I figured that part out." He had been over the maps of Edelweiss and the surrounding area hundreds of times. He knew a lake when it stared him in the face. He also knew the lake was over seventy-five feet deep. It was perfect for waterskiing, boating, and fishing. The residents who purchased his condominiums would find it highly entertaining during the summer months. Jordon didn't find the thought of skating on it the least bit entertaining. Only one man in history had ever managed the feat of walking on water, and it hadn't been he.

Gretchen tied the reins over a rail and pleasantly wished everyone a good time while casting quick glances at Jordon's scowling face. When they were alone in the shelter built for horses and sleighs, she asked, "Change your mind?"

Jordon pulled his morbid thoughts away from cracking ice and mustered a smile while jumping down from his perch. "No. I was just wondering how safe it is."

"It's perfectly safe. It's checked daily for thickness and more often than that if there are any sudden changes in temperature." She chuckled at his look of concentration. "Relax, Jordon, we haven't lost a skater yet." She hesitated a moment before impishly adding, "Except Boris Schoenberger, and he doesn't count."

"Why doesn't he count?" *How could a man's life not count?*

Gretchen headed out of the shelter. "He wasn't ice-skating at the time."

Jordon grabbed her elbow and turned her around to face him. Just as he suspected, she was laughing. "Gretchen?"

"Boris was one of the first settlers of Edelweiss. He had a reputation for being something of a ladies' man. One summer evening he took the banker's daughter, Greta, out to the lake for a little fast-and-loose." She studied Jordon's expression to make sure he had the picture. By his amused look, he did. "Poor Boris got more than he bargained for. Greta never uttered the word, no."

Repulsed, Jordon shuddered. "And they named it Lake Conquest after that?" *Some poor girl lost her innocence to a rogue, and for the rest of history a lake bore the name of her shame.*

"Lord, no," Gretchen said. "Greta was very satisfied with *her conquest*. She was the one who christened the lake. She brazenly walked into her home and told her father exactly what had happened. It seems Greta had been in love with Boris for years and was getting tired of his sowing wild oats. They were married within the month."

Jordon heard the proverbial door slamming behind Boris. "Did the marriage last?"

"Most definitely. They had twelve children and ninety-eight grandchildren." Jordon paled. "By all accounts Boris died within a week of Greta from a broken heart. Almost everyone living in Edelweiss today can trace their roots back to Boris and Greta."

"So how was he lost?"

"The remaining single and some of the married women of Edelweiss moaned his nuptial bliss quite openly."

Jordon chuckled and pulled her closer. "Are Boris and Greta sitting in your family tree?"

"They're one of the thickest branches."

He moved one of her skates from between them. Even with the plastic guard on, he wasn't trusting them. Her blue eyes sparkled with anticipation. "How many other males lost their independence on Lake Conquest?"

Her arms slid around his waist. "None that we know of. Everyone in this part of New Hampshire knows the legend."

"What legend?" His lips grazed her cheek.

"The seducer will end up being caught in his own trap for life."

Jordon nipped at her enticing lower lip. "I could think of worse punishments."

One brow rose in question. "Such as?" She silently cursed her red leather gloves as her arms slid up his back. She wanted to feel the rich texture of his hair between her fingers.

His mouth hovered above hers. "You uttering the word no." Jordon's mouth lowered the fraction of an inch needed to taste her warmth.

The kiss stole every one of her objections. Condominiums disappeared. Hundred-year-old legends faded from memory. The simple word *no* evaporated from her vocabulary. If sly Greta had felt one tenth of this chemistry when Boris kissed her, Gretchen could understand her brazen determination. Lake Conquest had been appropriately named.

Jordon broke the heated kiss as a group of skaters noisily made their way toward the shelter. Within a moment company would be arriving.

Gretchen hastily put some space between them as the guests from one of the bed and breakfasts in town pushed and jostled their way into the shelter looking for their sleigh.

A plump woman with rosy cheeks and a boisterous laugh stopped in midstride and glanced at Gretchen and then at Jordon. Rapid-fire German filled the shelter.

Jordon had no idea what the woman was saying, but he instinctively stepped protectively closer to Gretchen.

"No, Elise, everything is fine." Gretchen smiled up at Jordon's scowl. "This man is not bothering me."

Jordon's scowl turned into a look of outrage. What did this Elise person think, that he was some sort of pervert who lurked around horse stalls?

Elise beamed with pleasure and quickly loaded up her guests. As the sleigh passed Gretchen and Jordon, Elise called a warning in German.

"What did she say?" asked Jordon.

Gretchen laughed and led Jordon out of the shelter and toward the shed, where he could rent a pair of ice skates. "She told me to think of the legend." Her eyes sparkled with humor. "Boris was rumored to be a handsome devil too."

Jordon frowned and demanded, "Just who is seducing whom here?"

Gretchen batted her baby blues. Sugar could have melted in her mouth when she purred, "Really, Jordon, I don't know what you're talking about."

Minutes later Jordon stared from his skate-clad feet to the lake's edge, ten feet away. He was never going to make it. A swarm of skaters were busily gliding, jumping, and whipping their way across the ice. Six huge bonfires were spaced around a small area of the lake. Gretchen had explained that skating was restricted to this portion of the lake only for safety reasons. A small trailer sold hot chocolate and hot buttered rum, complete with a cinnamon stick. Jordon was dying to try the buttered rum; his fingers were starting to freeze.

"Come on, Wobbly, if you don't start moving, you'll freeze solid."

Jordon glanced at Gretchen standing in front of him. Her red cape billowed around her calves. How was she ever going to skate in that? "Why don't you show me how it's done?"

Gretchen arched a finely tipped brow as understanding dawned. He didn't think she could skate in this coat. Well, hell, no one could skate in this billowing contraption. She had worn it for warmth, not to skate in. "Okay, you sit right there and pay close attention." With a teasing smile she lowered the hood and unbuttoned the three shoulder buttons holding the cape closed.

Jordon swallowed hard as Gretchen slid gracefully out of the cape and draped it over the back of the chair. Her hair was braided and tied with a simple rubber band. A turquoise sweater was paired with a black turtleneck top and a short black-and-turquoise skirt flared around the top of her thighs. Thick black tights clung to her shapely legs, and a pair of blinding-white ice skates adorned her dainty feet.

"I'll be right back."

Heat poured through his veins like one-hundred-proof bourbon as she turned around and gracefully made her way to the ice. The temperature in Edelweiss was climbing rapidly. Shouldn't someone check the thickness of the ice? He noticed she waved and greeted several people as she slowly glided through the crowd, heading for open spaces. Numerous male heads turned in appreciation as she gracefully sailed back and forth. By her fourth pass she was adding simple jumps and turns. Five minutes later she had acquired a small audience and Jordon's admiration. She was as graceful on skates as she was on skis.

By the time she rejoined him at the bench, she was out of breath, but he was the one breathing heavily. His jacket was unzipped, and he had moved to the edge of the wooden bench. Hot, bold need was pressing heavily against his jeans. Tantalizing glimpses of her pert bottom covered in turquoise panties had caused more than his blood pressure to skyrocket. "I hope you don't expect me to try one of those jumps."

She heard the hard edge of desire thickening his voice. A smile played at the corner of her mouth as she reached out her hand to help him to his feet. "No, Jordon. With you I'm going to have to go really slow."

Gretchen continued her pacing around the monstrous thing sitting in the middle of her living room. She beseechingly glanced at the woman who came running up to her apartment in response to her hysterical phone call. "Effie, he bought me a tree!"

Effie puffed out her ample bosom and grinned. "It's not a tree, *liebchen*. It's a weeping fig plant."

"Lord, it's going to grow fruit!" Gretchen immediately took two steps backward. What in the world was she supposed to do with figs? Can them? Or as her grandmother called it, "put them up"? Where exactly her grandmother put them up to was down in the basement. So why it was called "putting them up" was a mystery to her. The only time she had ever eaten figs was in cookies, and then all they did was stick to her teeth and make her thirsty. Jordon had an odd sense of romance. When she had entered her apartment moments earlier, she nearly had heart failure at finding a five-foot-plus tree in her living room. Jordon's note had been tied with a mint-colored ribbon around the trunk. *How about green? See you at dessert. "J."* P.S. *Next time lock your door to the supply room. Any crazy could have gotten in here.* The warning came too late—some crazy already had come in and started the forest in her living room.

"Weeping figs don't bear fruit."

Grateful for that piece of information, Gretchen asked, "What do I do now?"

Effie looked at Gretchen and clicked her tongue. "I would say, thank Mr. Winters."

"I know that." She gently touched one of the shiny green leaves and was surprised when it didn't disintegrate in her hand. "I mean with the tree. Do I water it or what?"

Understanding dawned in Effie's eyes as she glanced around the room. Besides a bouquet of yellow roses sitting on the coffee table, the room held no other plants. "You don't have any plants?"

"Oh, I have plants, all right. Fourteen pots of violets, not counting my shade tree here." She saw Effie glance around the room again and sighed. "They're in the bathtub."

Effie walked down the hall. Within moments she was back, slowly shaking her head. "They're going to die in there."

Gretchen sat on the couch and absentmindedly picked up a yellow rose petal. Why hadn't Jordon stuck to sending cut flowers? At least when they faded and died she wouldn't feel responsible.

"Smile, *liebchen,* all they need is light." Effie walked through her entire apartment studying the views from the different windows and glass doors.

Fifteen minutes later the smile was back on Gretchen's face. The violets were on an old table from the storage room basking in the late-afternoon light streaming into her bedroom from the glass doors. With a little repositioning of her living-room furniture the fig tree had found a home close to the doors leading to the balcony without being in the way.

Effie handed her a detailed list on when and how much to water the plants and the promise to return every other day to check on their condition. "Now, you go and get dressed into something special for that man of yours."

"He's not my man."

Effie snorted and opened the door. "The only thing I haven't figured out is why fourteen violets?"

"Because that's how many steps there are." Gretchen answered as she pushed the bewildered woman out of the door.

Jordon slowly stirred his coffee and watched as Gretchen dashed back into the kitchen. Their dessert was still sitting untouched on his table. He had been waiting for thirty minutes. The woman worked too hard. This morning when he had come down for breakfast, she was already behind the closed door of her office. He had been tempted to knock, but he was afraid she was reading over his proposal, and then he would have to act the part of president of Winters Enterprises. He was beginning to despise Winters Enterprises and the rift it was causing between Gretchen and himself. He could read it in her eyes. She was still unsure about his motive.

The temptation to renege on the land option was overwhelming. That would prove, without a shadow of doubt, that he wasn't attracted to her because she held the position of being Edelweiss's mayor. Two things stopped him. Business ethics was the first. If one of his employees purposely jeopardized a business deal, they'd be walking the streets by nightfall. Winters Enterprises might bear his name, but he didn't have the right to abuse his staff's loyalty or respect. Second, and more important, he wanted Gretchen's trust. Some joker had done an incredible job smashing her confidence as a woman.

The tempo of his heartbeat increased a notch as

Gretchen stepped back into the room. She glanced around and seemed to be satisfied. Half the tables were now empty, and the guests remaining all appeared to be lingering over dessert and coffee. Her dark-green skirt swayed enticingly as she made her way to his table. He noticed a few male heads turn to appreciate the view. He slowly stood, silently stating his claim, and waited for her. The woman obviously had no notion of her appeal.

She smiled her thanks as Jordon politely held out her chair.

"You're working too hard." He frowned as Peter approached the table and placed a full plate in front of Gretchen. "You haven't had dinner yet?"

Gretchen thanked Peter and picked up her fork. "You don't mind if I eat now, do you?"

"Of course not." He glanced at his watch; it was after nine. "Is it always this busy on a Saturday night?"

She swallowed. "Sometimes it's worse." She had run around for the past three hours to make sure everything was running smoothly, and now she was free for the rest of the night. Pride lightened her voice as she said, "The bed-and-breakfast establishments in town only offer breakfast, so the Dragon's Lair usually handles their guests, plus the day-trippers."

"Day-trippers?"

"Skiers who come only for the day. They spend their days on the slopes and the evening in town before driving back to wherever they came from."

"Maybe you should think about opening another restaurant."

Gretchen looked up from her meal and frowned. He was serious. "Jordon, the Dragon's Lair gets a trifle hectic only on Saturday nights during the ski season. How would this other restaurant support itself the rest of the time?"

"Tourism."

She could follow this conversation to it logical conclusion, with the two of them butting heads over the growth of Edelweiss; or she could change the subject before it ruined the evening. "Possibly." She picked up her coffee. "I haven't gotten the chance to thank you properly for the tree."

"The florist assured me it was a plant, not a tree." Heat coiled low in his stomach. Last night she had thanked him for the violets with fourteen luscious, toe-curling kisses on her doorstep. A humorous smile curved his mouth. "Are you going to thank me now?"

She glanced around the room at the dozen or so remaining guests. She contemplated her answer.

Jordon's heart nearly exploded when he saw her expression. She was thinking about it! Trust was taking a giant step forward. Tenderness pooled in his eyes. "Why don't you thank me later?"

Relief and frustration battled within her. "There's a band playing in the lounge tonight."

Slow dancing with Gretchen wrapped in his arms sounded like heaven. "I'll take you dancing only after you clean your plate."

Gretchen's smile held pure magic as she dug into her meal.

Six

Jordon took the key to the apartment from Gretchen's trembling fingers and unlocked the door. Maybe dancing hadn't been such a good idea. His body was so aroused, the mere fragrance of her hair was about to send him over the edge. His control had disappeared by the second slow dance, and he was frightened Gretchen would realize how much he wanted her and barricade herself on top of Thunder Mountain with her mythical dragons as protectors.

"Would you like to come in for a cup of coffee?"

His hand tightened its crushing grip on the doorjamb. Last night he hadn't been invited in after his first skating lesson. Last night he might have been able to control this fiery desire. Tonight, after holding her in his arms and softly swaying to the music, there wasn't a chance in hell he could. Gretchen had allowed him a glimpse of her heart, and he saw the trust shining there. He couldn't break that trust. "If I come in, it won't be for coffee."

Gretchen studied his features illuminated in the shadowy hallway. She wanted him. If she was being so honest with herself, she might as well admit to wanting him ever since he walked her home from the beer festival. The condominiums had thrown her momentarily off balance. She had been allowing Tom's betrayal to rule her life. Jordon was not Tom. Jordon had purposely brought up the condos before anything developed between them. He had been straightforward and honest with his declaration. She had been equally blunt in her reply.

She still wanted him.

"That's good. I ran out of coffee the last time you were here."

Jordon forgot to inhale. His fingers loosened their stranglehold on the woodwork and tenderly cupped her flushed cheek. "Do you have any idea what you're asking?"

"Yes." She pressed her cheek deeper into his palm. She could feel the slight trembling of his hand. "I'm asking you to stay."

He lowered his head. "Oh, lady"—his lips brushed hers—"try keeping me away now." His mouth settled firmly on her satisfied smile.

Gretchen surrendered to the demand of his kiss. Her arms encircled his neck. Black silken strands of his hair intertwined with her pale fingers. Desire roared through her body like a flash flood, devastating every nerve ending in its path. This is where she belonged in life, in Jordon's arms. Nothing that felt this right could possibly be wrong, she thought as he picked her up and carried her into the apartment.

Jordon held fast to his precious bundle as he closed the door, sealing them from the outside world. His tongue plunged deeper into the cherished sweetness of her mouth as he released her legs and suffered the torment of Gretchen's luscious curves slowly sliding down his throbbing body. His free hand tunneled through her hair and started to pluck the pins holding the golden mass into a bun.

Gretchen interlocked her fingers behind his neck and gloried in every hard inch of Jordon as her feet slid to the floor. Standing on tiptoes with her skirt bunched around her thighs, she heatedly met his tongue and challenged him. Her full breasts strained the confines of her white blouse to press against his chest.

Jordon groaned as her hair tumbled to her waist. He released her mouth and buried his face within the golden haven. He breathed in a delicate floral scent mixed with a clean, brisk aroma. She smelled as if she had been skiing down a mountain of wildflowers. He wondered if the erotic fragrance was elsewhere on her body.

His lips fastened on the thunderous pulse beating in her slender neck as his hand curved around one breast and his leg wedged between hers. He shuddered as a nipple blossomed in his palm. "Gretchen, what are you doing to me?"

He should have known he wouldn't be able to control it. All the signs had been there. Whatever was happening between them was too powerful to be contained by civilized proprieties, he thought as he undid her buttons.

Gretchen felt the cool smoothness of the door against her back as the blouse slipped over her shoulders, then shivered when Jordon's lips captured a nipple through the filmy lace of her white bra.

"Jordon?" Her voice held the frustration of having her arms pinned to the door by her sleeves. She needed to touch him.

"Hmmm . . ." He laved the other stiff peak with his tongue.

"Jordon!"

The urgency in her voice penetrated his passionate, dazed mind. He released his treasure and looked up.

She leaned her head back and indicated her bound arms. "I don't know about you"—she blew a wisp of hair away from her eyes—"but I usually don't go for bondage."

He stared, appalled at her predicament. He was ready to take her pinned against the front door. Her blouse was halfway off, and moist circles darkened the delicate lace of her bra. Yards of dark-green material were draped across his leg, and the heels of her black boots were scuffing the white door. His gaze returned to her face, expecting to find fear. What he saw was arousal. Her cheeks were flushed, she was breathing rapidly, and the gleam of sexual frustration shimmered in her eyes.

A slow smile curved his mouth. She wanted her hands free to participate. With renewed patience he used his tongue to outline the pulse beating under the surface of her satin-smooth throat. "You don't, huh?" With his teeth he lowered the slim straps of her bra. He moaned as her soft breasts rubbed against his jaw.

"Jordon, please!" She rocked her hips against the straining muscles on his leg.

He repaid the compliment by trailing a fiery blaze of kisses down her throat and over the gentle swelling spilling out of the lace. He ended with moist kisses in the shadowy depths between the twin mounds. "Please, what?" He held her slim waist with both of his hands and grinned.

Gretchen banged her fists against the door. "Wait until I get my hands on you!"

His chuckle filled the room as he swept her up into his arms. "Oh, Gretchen, can't you see, that's the problem?" His long strides closed the distance between the living-room door and her bedroom in an instant. "I can't wait for your hands to be on me."

Moonlight filled the room with a pale glow. Jordon slowly lowered her near the foot of the bed. His gaze never left her exquisite face. He wanted to remember every expression she made the first time they made love.

Gretchen regained her balance and quickly unbuttoned the cuffs of her blouse. She smiled in triumph as it slipped free of her arms and drifted to the floor. Her hands reached for the hem of his sweater. "I want to touch you." She felt the shudder that shook his body. Her eyes locked with his gaze, and her whisper carried the promise of paradise. "Everywhere."

The tables had been turned. Jordon found himself on the pleading end. "Please." His hands covered hers as he helped pulled the sweater over his head.

Her fingers trembled as she worked the small white buttons of his shirt. Her bra joined the discarded sweater and blouse. Her breath caught as she spread open his shirt and glimpsed the black curls that swirled across his chest. Her palms flattened in fascination against his muscular chest. Black curls wrapped around her fingers and held them captive.

Jordon shrugged out of his shirt as hot fingers danced over his body. He lifted her hands and

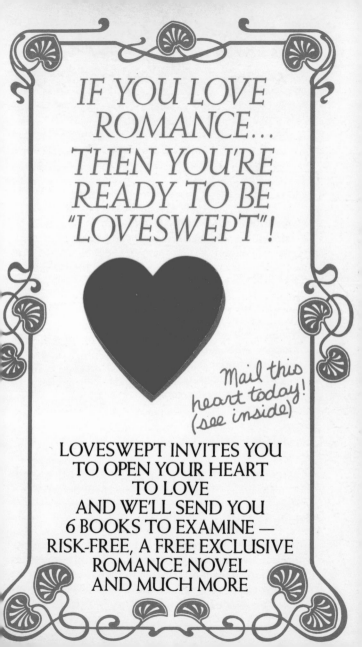

IF YOU LOVE
ROMANCE...
THEN YOU'RE
READY TO BE
"LOVESWEPT"!

*Mail this
heart today!
(see inside)*

LOVESWEPT INVITES YOU
TO OPEN YOUR HEART
TO LOVE
AND WE'LL SEND YOU
6 BOOKS TO EXAMINE —
RISK-FREE, A FREE EXCLUSIVE
ROMANCE NOVEL
AND MUCH MORE

OPEN YOUR HEART TO LOVE
YOU'LL BE LOVESWEPT WITH THIS OFFER!

HERE'S WHAT YOU GET:

1. **RISK-FREE!** SIX NEW LOVESWEPT NOVELS! Preview 6 beautiful stories filled with passion, romance, laughter and tears . . . exciting romances to stir the excitement of falling in love . . . again and again.

2. **FREE!** AN EXCLUSIVE ROMANCE NOVEL! You'll receive *Larger Than Life* by the best-selling author Kay Hooper ABSOLUTELY FREE. You won't find it in bookstores anywhere. Instead, it's reserved for you as our way of saying "thank you."

3. **SAVE!** MONEY-SAVING HOME DELIVERY! Join the Loveswept at-home reader service and we'll send you 6 new novels each month. You always get 15 days to preview them before you decide whether to keep it. Each book is yours for only $2.25 — a savings of 54¢ per book.

4. **BEAT THE CROWDS!** You'll always receive your Loveswept books before they are available in bookstores. You'll be the first to thrill to these exciting new stories.

BE LOVESWEPT TODAY — JUST COMPLETE, DETACH AND MAIL YOUR RISK-FREE ORDER CARD

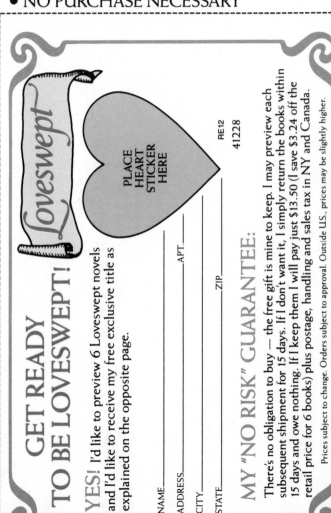

REMEMBER!

- The free gift is mine to keep!
- There is no obligation!
- I may preview each shipment for 15 days!
- I may cancel anytime!

placed them around his neck. Her fingers immediately went into his hair. In awe he gazed at her dusky-tipped pale breasts. They seemed to be pouting for his attention. He placed a light kiss on each nipple. "You're more beautiful than I imagined."

She pulled him closer and buried the sensitive peaks deep within the dark, curling mass. Her head was thrown back and eyes were closed in ecstasy. "It wasn't this good in my dreams."

His lips found the creamy area behind her ear. "Did you dream of me?"

She drew his mouth to hers. Her answer feathered his lips. "For years, Jordon. For years."

The kiss was explosive in its need.

Hunger met hunger. Hands pushed, pulled, and caressed away their remaining clothes. Moans of pleasure and words of praise tumbled off lips to be murmured against glistening flesh. The last barrier of silk slid down Gretchen's legs. With a delicate kick she sent the scrap of silk flying as Jordon lifted her back into his arms.

He laid her down in the middle of the red comforter. Her golden hair shone with moonlight, and her arms reached for him. "Beautiful." He placed a fleeting kiss on each outstretched palm.

Gretchen stroked his slightly abrasive jaw with the tips of her fingers. "Yes, beautiful." She gently brushed the outline of his ears before sinking her hands into his hair and pulling his mouth down. A sweet, faint purr escaped into his mouth as his body pressed her into the bed.

She shifted her legs to cradle his hips. He groaned and twisted his mouth away from her. "We have to slow down." His fingers squeezed her hip trying to hold it still. They were going too fast.

He was ready to plunge into her depths heedless of her pleasure.

Her tongue found a nipple under a thatch of curls. She lightly blew on the moist nub. "Why?"

Jordon's grip tightened as another bout of need rocketed through his body. "I want this to last."

Smooth, pale legs rubbed against strong, rough hairy thighs, enticing him closer. She could feel the weight of his arousal. Her voice was breathless with anticipation. "Next time."

He reached between them to test her readiness. Moist heat coated his finger. He bit his lower lip and slid a second finger in. He groaned as her silken walls contracted around him. Awed by her response, he muttered, "You are ready."

She arched her hips, glorifying in the feel of him, but wanting more. "I've been ready."

He removed his fingers and lightly nipped her seductive lower lip. He cupped a creamy breast and traced the darkened peak with his tongue. "Since when?" He savored the other nipple and gently nudged his throbbing arousal at the heart of her heat. "Could I have taken you against the door?"

Her legs wrapped around the back of his thighs as he slowly filled her and moved within her. Small convulsions signaled the beginning of her climax. Her hot tightening broke his control. He pulled back and thrust deep into her with a wild rhythm.

His shout of release was muffled against her throat.

Dainty fingers lightly caressed his slick back as she murmured, "Oh, yes," over and over.

Jordon woke up to the golden light of dawn and the painful tightening of his chest. His eyes focused in on the cause of the pain. A pink-tipped hand had a solid grip on his chest hair. His gaze followed the graceful curve of her arm past her shoulder to Gretchen's face. She was cradled in his arms, using his shoulder for a pillow, and his chest hair for a security blanket.

The woman was fascinated with the textures of his hair. If her fingers weren't sunk into his hair, she was weaving them across his chest. Desire twisted in his gut as he remembered the other patch of hair that interested her. It had been her fascination that initiated their second round of lovemaking. She had been wrong when she said the next time would be slower. Only an official stopwatch could have measured the difference.

He covered her fist with his hand and gently released the caught hair. His sigh of relief ruffled her hair as she snuggled closer and tunneled her fingers back into the black curls. This time she didn't pull.

He glanced around the room with interest. Twin double doors, matching those in the living room, led out to a snow-covered balcony. Thunder Mountain glistened in the near distance capturing the first rays of the morning sun. From his position on the bed he couldn't see its peak. A white area rug, scattered with their clothing, was stretched across a hardwood floor. A lone red Queen Anne chair and a marble-top table sat by one set of patio doors. The dozen red roses he had given her were in the center of the table. A black-lacquered armoire adorned with twin elegant dragons virtually took up one wall. A fireplace, which looked unused, graced the wall between the glass doors, and fourteen lavender violets jock-eyed for position on a low table in front of the other door. The sheets were black satin, and the down-filled comforter was of the highest quality and shimmered in its redness.

Curious, he turned his head to get a better look at the bed and froze. He was being stared at.

An angry green scaled dragon was flashing his golden claws and menacing teeth. Its fiery red mane glistened in the pale morning light. Two topaz eyes blazed to life as the sun's rays captured the beauty of the gemstones. The exquisite beast was carved and painted into a five-foot headboard of solid teak. He had been sleeping in a work of art.

"I see you've met Chung." Gretchen's voice was rough with sleep.

Jordon returned his attention to the warm woman in his arms. He had been so startled by the dragon, he hadn't realized she had awakened. "Morning." He brushed his lips over hers. "You named your bed?"

She yawned again. "Just the headboard." She loved how he looked in the morning. All tousled, rough, and naked.

"There's one thing I don't understand." He stilled as Gretchen slid a leg over his. His voice dropped an octave. "Why the eastern decor?"

Her questing fingers felt a hardening nipple. "I lived and worked in San Francisco, near China-town, for five years." She placed a string of kisses over his collarbone. "Chung's an eastern dragon. It is his duty in life to guard." Her tongue swept over the deep V at the base of his throat. "Since I bought him, he has to guard me."

Jordon shifted his position as her seductive mouth branded him. His breathing quickened and his hand skimmed down her back to lovingly cup her bottom. He had no idea what the conversation was about. "Guard you from what?"

"Mountain predators." She slid her leg over his other one, shifted her weight, and straddled him. His thick arousal greeted the dewy softness between her thighs. "They're the dragons who feed off the weaknesses in people."

He had wanted to go slowly with Gretchen this morning. He needed to know it wasn't just the heat of the night that caused the sensations bombarding his senses. Nothing like last night had ever happened before in his life, and he had the feeling it would never repeat itself with anyone but this woman. He had been attracted to other women before, but this feeling went beyond attraction. He needed the name of this new emotion.

Jordon leaned up and captured one of her pouting nipples between his lips. The temptation was too great. His hands gripped her hips and lifted. Her low sigh of pleasure curled his toes as he slowly filled her.

Later he would regain the control over his body. Later he would make slow and sweet love to Gretchen. Later he would name this curious emotion filling his soul.

Gretchen buried her head farther under the pillow to block out the light. She needed sleep. She needed a shower. She tried to swallow and groaned. Right then she would sell her most prized possession, Chung, on the black market for a cup of coffee. She cautiously moved her foot. All it encountered was warm satin sheets. Jordon was gone.

She peeked out from under the pillow and frowned. Disappointment flared at the sight of the empty bed. She glanced at the clock and groaned.

It was after nine. She never slept this late. Who was running the Dragon's Lair?

The distinct smell of coffee drifted into the room. Somewhere in her apartment was coffee. She would recognize that smell anywhere. Impossible. She had been telling the truth to Jordon when she said she had run out the other day.

Curious, she slipped out of bed, pulled on the white silk robe hanging on the back of the bathroom door, and padded barefoot out to the kitchen. A smile lit her face. Jordon was standing in the middle of the room dividing a tray of food into two equal parts. A pot of coffee sat on the tray.

His hair was still damp from a recent shower, and he was wearing different clothes from the previous night. He had obviously gone back to his room and, by the looks of things, ordered a big enough breakfast for two. He would have raised more than a few eyebrows by ordering breakfast for two sent to her apartment. Jordon was a gentleman. Her heart swelled with the knowledge that he was not one to kiss and tell.

Jordon turned around, spotted Gretchen, and grinned. "You're up."

"I'm not officially up until I've had my shower and two cups of coffee." She walked into the room and poured a cup from the insulated pitcher on the tray.

Warm masculine arms wrapped around her waist and pulled her back against him. Cool silk ran through his fingers as he played with the sash of her robe. The garment was pure snow white with a furious dragon embroidered with glittering red thread across the back. And if his teasing fingers were right, it was the only thing she had on.

Gretchen leaned into his strength as she sipped

the dark brew. The morning had definitely taken a turn for the better since waking up in bed alone. She took another sip of coffee, tilted her face to see him, and smiled.

His hands instinctively tightened. She was sleepy-eyed, rumpled, and the most incredibly sexy woman in the world. She was also in his arms smiling a very satisfied grin. "Are you up yet?"

She rubbed her bottom against the front of his trousers. "I see I'm not the only one."

Jordon laughed and lowered his head for a kiss. "I promised myself I was going to behave this morning."

Gretchen placed her cup on the counter and reached for him. "You should always prepare a lady for such a disappointment."

He chuckled. She was turning into one surprise after another. From the poised innkeeper to a wildly passionate woman, and now a teasing minx. His kiss was light and brief. "Our breakfast is getting cold."

Gretchen frowned and stepped out of his arms.

He picked up the tray and carried it to the table. "Where's a food store around here?"

She carried her cup over and sat down. "Why?" What in the world could he possibly want with a food store?

"I didn't like leaving your bed to sneak back to my room to order from room service." He smiled at her dazed expression. "I only did it this morning because I wasn't sure how you would react to your staff knowing I spent the night with you." He leaned forward and poured more coffee into her cup. "I don't plan on repeating that trip tomorrow morning."

Her heart zinged in ecstasy. He was planning on

spending another night. "I could pick up some food later."

"No, I'll do it. I have to go into town anyway." He dug into his food. When he reached for his cup, he noticed she hadn't touched a thing on her plate. She was sitting there staring at him with a peculiar expression on her face. "What's wrong?"

Gretchen blinked. *What's wrong?* How could she tell him what she had only just discovered for herself? She was falling in love with him. She had been sitting here pushing scrambled eggs around her plate when, bam!—there it was. Why hadn't someone warned her that it could happen within the blink of an eye, or that breakfast wasn't only the most important meal of the day, it could also be the most hazardous. She could have been swallowing a hunk of toast when the reality of the situation hit her. She would have been the first person to die because she fell in love. Lord, what if thousands of people died each year from the shock and no one knew? What if she'd been driving a car?

"Gretchen?" Jordon didn't like the way the color was draining out of her face. She looked ready to pass out.

She dropped her fork and primly folded her hands. She wasn't going to take any chances while the shock was still ricocheting through her body. She'd never truly fallen in love before, and the idea of not living long enough to see it to the end was disturbing. With Tom the relationship had developed over months of working together. The physical side had been satisfying. At the time she had thought it was love. Now she was beginning to understand she hadn't the faintest idea what love was all about. She still didn't. How could she fall in love with a man who wanted to change her town? Their viewpoints were coming from opposite ends of the universe. Everything she had built and worked for was sitting in Edelweiss. This was her life. Jordon's life was in New York City, which might as well be the other end of the universe.

Jordon's hands covered her trembling fingers. "Are you all right, Gretchen?"

"Fine." Her voice squeaked like a mouse. She cleared her throat and tried again. "Fine."

He stared hard at her face. "Don't you want me to spend another night?"

"I . . ." She couldn't tell him no, even if breaking this attraction now, before it turned from falling-to-rock-bottom, death-do-us-part love would be the smartest thing to do. She needed to know how far it would grow. Loneliness had plagued her life for so long now, she needed the feeling of completeness only his arms seemed able to give. "I don't like eggs."

Jordon had followed every conflicting emotion that flitted across her face. Her anxiety tore at his heart. He knew he had pushed too hard, too fast, but hell, he had never felt like this before. He was scared she'd have regrets or doubts, and she was. Still they obviously weren't that strong, or she would have shown him the door.

His glance shifted to the door and he couldn't help smiling at the memory. She was like gunpowder to his fuse. Mix the two together and wham!—instant explosion.

Gretchen nervously shifted on the chair as the color red swept up her cheeks. She had followed Jordon's gaze.

"I love that door," Jordon muttered.

She swallowed the humiliation and scowled at the twin heel marks her boots had caused, about twelve inches off the ground. "It needs to be painted."

"Hell, woman!" Jordon shouted horrified at the thought. "It needs to be bronzed."

Gretchen giggled at the thought of bronzing the entire door. It would weigh a ton. "I'll never be able to get back in."

Jordon's thumb lightly drew circles on the back of her hand. "You mean, you would never be able to get out." His fingers detected the rapid increase in her pulse. "The more I think of it, the better I like that idea."

"Getting the door bronzed?" Her hand had melted in his grip. There wasn't a bone left in it.

"No." He picked up her hand and pressed his lips to the soft white palm. "The thought of keeping you trapped in this apartment." His gaze dropped from the bottomless pools in her eyes to the lapels of her robe. They had gaped far enough to offer him an enticing display of cleavage. But it was the bountiful mounds hidden in the shadowy depths that had him enthralled. Had it really been only hours since he had tasted their fruit? It seemed like a lifetime.

Gretchen felt the sensitive peaks of her breasts go rigid from his glance. "Don't you think I'll be lonely?"

His tongue traced her a line on her palm and brushed across the rapidly beating pulse in her wrist. His gaze settled on her slightly parted lips. "Lonely is one thing you'd never be."

"Oh, will I have company?"

"Morning." He nipped playfully at the base of her thumb. "Noon." His teeth grazed her index finger. "And night." He gently drew the tip of her middle finger into his mouth and sucked.

Moisture gathered between her thighs. It was

criminal how easy Jordon could make her want him. "It's morning now."

Jordon closed his eyes and willed himself to release her hand. Five minutes ago she had had doubts about them. He was not going to use sex to hold her. Granted, it wasn't just sex, nothing that wild and consuming could be classified as just plain sex. He was a mature man. Thirty-eight-year-old men didn't go around using sex as a lure. He glanced at the twin peaks pressing outward from beneath her robe and groaned. Maybe they did. How was he supposed to know what other men did? At this moment he couldn't remember what he did yesterday. He glanced at Gretchen's mouth. Every detail from last night and dawn came rushing back. If he didn't get her out of there soon, he was going to embarrass himself by begging. "Don't you have to take a shower or something?"

Gretchen yanked her hand back to her side of the table. "Well, you don't have to get personal about it." Her chair scraped the floor as she stood up. She knew she didn't look her best first thing in the morning. What woman did?

"Gretchen!" Jordon barked. "I could lay you across this table right this minute and eat you for breakfast."

She read the honesty and heat in his gaze.

"I'm trying to be noble and give you some time to get to know me." His smile was a little self-conscious. "I have it on good authority that I can be arrogant, overbearing, and possessive of what's mine."

She leaned against the doorjamb, folded her arms under her breasts, and silently contemplated the faults he'd just recited. "Who was the *good authority*—wife or girlfriend?"

Jordon shrugged. "Neither, it was my mother."

Gretchen chuckled. She would personally like to shake Mrs. Winters's hand. The lady had guts. Since he was being so forthright, she decided to return the favor. "I'm independent, slightly untrusting, and I try never to show any signs of weakness."

The independence was admirable, and the part about untrusting he would handle later. "Why never display your weakness?"

Her hand waved absently toward the ceiling. "They're out there waiting to pounce."

"Who?"

"The dragons of the world." She pushed away from the door and clutched the lapels of the robe together. "Remember I told you about the mountain predators and how they feed off the weaknesses in people?"

Jordon squinted his eyes as he studied Gretchen. She wasn't making much sense. How much did he really know about the real Gretchen. "Real dragons?"

Gretchen slowly shook her head. Jordon didn't understand. "No, Jordon, there aren't any such creatures left, if they ever existed at all." She tried to explain it better. "Dragons are what we make them. They can be good, such as Chung, or they can be mountain predators. If you show your weaknesses and admit your fears, they would hone in on them and strike. If a person was afraid of dying, they would use that fear. If a person had claustrophobia, every time that person was stuck in a tight space, those mountain predators would be there."

Jordon nodded his head as understanding started to dawn. She wasn't crazy, she just had a different way of looking at things. "What are you most afraid of, Gretchen?"

She looked at the man who had stolen a chunk of her heart. If she was ever going to fight the mountain predators in her life, she had to start somewhere. It might as well be with the man she was falling in love with. "That I will live my entire life and never once be true to myself."

She silently watched as bewilderment clouded Jordon's expression. She couldn't blame him; she didn't fully understand it herself. With a slight droop to her shoulders she turned and headed for her shower.

Seven

Gretchen got out of the passenger's side of Jordon's car and followed his footprints up the hill. She didn't want to be here. In fact she would rather have been anywhere in Edelweiss with Jordon than here. Crisp snow crunched under her boots as she trudged her way up the incline.

Her breath was frosty wisps on the wind as she joined Jordon at the crest. His hands were deep in the pockets of his new coat. Blue denim outlined his legs while his new boots received their first christening of snow. His eyes seem to be searching the breathtaking view for an answer. She knew he wouldn't find it.

Gretchen duplicated his pose and searched for her own answers. The Beckers' chimney was sending up a gentle swirl of smoke. The deep snow had melted in a few places, especially around the barn where a few stray cows had ventured outside. Their driveway had been plowed, but the fields were buried beneath a white winter blanket.

Shadow Mountain stretched endlessly upward

from the sloping fields, and Thunder Mountain stood majestically in the distance. The ski slopes were doing brisk business for a Tuesday. Edelweiss laid protectively cradled between the two. She could pick out Main Street and possibly the dot that was William Tell's statue. Had her only worry a week ago really been that Claus would somehow manage to sway the council to move the statue? Oh, how life fools the unsuspecting.

She was tired of life happening to her; she wanted to make a happening in it. She glanced sideways at the pensive man beside her. "Why did you bring me here?"

He didn't look at her as he continued to survey the surroundings. "It's between us."

Gretchen looked again. Was he seeing what was there, or what would be there if he got his wish? Pristine fields would disappear under the weight of towering condominiums. Black, serpentine roads would snake their way across, around, and over the valley, giving the rich the fastest and easiest access to wherever they were going. Lake Conquest would be crowded with docks and boats of every color and size. A sporting-goods store would have to be built close by, along with a new bait shop. Who would want to drive all the way back into town to Erik's Sports Shop for bait? It would be a whole three miles out of their way.

She couldn't do it, not even for Jordon. "I'm sorry, Jordon. Even after reading all those reports, statistics, and spreadsheets I still can't allow you to do it."

A small smile touched his lips. He was disappointed she hadn't agreed. They could have settled the whole thing between them and got on with their lives. But in a way he was glad she was still sticking to her guns. He would never have been totally convinced that she hadn't gone against her principles because of what they shared in bed. The past three nights of sharing her bed had shown him how great that pull might be. He daily fought the temptation to scrap the entire project.

It was time for her to explain why she was so hesitant to hand out her trust. "What did he do to you?"

"Who?"

"The man from San Francisco. The one who taught you to be so untrusting." He watched the smoke curling out of the Beckers' chimney.

Gretchen squinted against the morning sun and gazed at Thunder Mountain. Not a dragon in sight. Maybe it was time to reveal one of her weaknesses and wave it like a red cape in front of the bull. If one of life's dragons were going to charge, it might as well be now. "His name was Tom. We worked for the same hotel chain. In the five years I worked there, I managed to move up the ranks quickly. Tom was relatively new to the organization, and he had a lot of ambition.

"After months of working closely together he . . . well"—she took a deep breath—"he moved in with me." There, she had said it. It wasn't one of the highlights in her life. She had gone against everything she believed in by living with a man out of wedlock. Her grandmother would have turned over in her grave if she had known. Gretchen had acted out everyone else's concept of what a business woman in the eighties was supposed to be and had tossed aside her dreams of a white wedding and a houseful of children.

Jordon slid a sideways glance at her. She had revealed more about herself by what she omitted than by what she was saying. Gretchen hadn't been true to herself when she was living with this Tom character. Was that the reason she never offered any closet space to him? His clothes were still kept in the room he rented at the inn.

"We lived together for nearly a year. He never seemed to mind that I was higher up or made more money."

Jordon could see where this was all heading. Her uncertainties stemmed from a bad relationship, one that had mixed business with pleasure. The exact thing they were doing now.

She kicked at the snow surrounding her feet. "I came home early one night and heard him on the phone giving confidential information to a competing business. That information was on computer files he had had no access to. He had to have used my codes to retrieve them."

Jordon growled, "He used you!" His hands clutched into fists as an offensive thought occurred to him. "Just as you think I'm using you."

"No." She scanned the blue skies. No predators had come to feed off her weakness. "You're nothing like Tom. The same rules don't pertain to you. You were honest and straightforward from the beginning. I knew exactly what you wanted."

"What *exactly* do you think I want?"

Gretchen glanced around at the impressive view. "You want the town council and me to give you the go-ahead with your condominiums."

"Is that all you think I want?" His voice was strained.

She looked from the Beckers' farm to Jordon's stony expression. "You want more?" What else could he expect Edelweiss to give up?

"You're damn right I want more." He closed the space between them and grabbed her shoulders. "I want it all!"

Her face paled. "Edelweiss?"

"No, Gretchen, I don't give a tinker's damn about Edelweiss. It's you I want. I want your independence and trust. I want you to be true to yourself." He gave her a gentle shake. "I want it all!"

Happiness lit up her face. *He wanted her, not the building permits!* Visions of a sumptuous wedding gown, complete with yards and yards of lace flashed through her mind. She imagined Jordon standing there holding a toddler, with tousled black hair and sparkling gray eyes. She imagined him patting her stomach, telling her he still loved her no matter how many dress sizes she went through and that pickles and ice cream sounded just fine for dinner. She threw her arms around Jordon and kissed him.

Jordon was momentarily knocked off balance by her heated kiss, but managed to make an astonishing comeback. When the ice beneath their feet was in danger of melting, he regrettably ended the kiss. "I take it you like that idea."

Gretchen ran her finger down the zipper of his jacket and toyed with the lift tickets. She had been so pleased when he told her he was taking private ski lessons during the day while she worked. The man knew the way to her heart. He'd even continued sending her flowers daily. How could she not help falling totally and completely in love with the man? She reached up and captured his mouth in a short kiss. "Thank you."

"You're welcome." He caught a wisp of hair the wind had blown across her face and tucked it behind her ear. "What was the thank-you for anyway?"

"Dropping the option on the Beckers' property."

Jordon released her as if she had burnt him. "What are you talking about?"

"You said that you wanted me and didn't give a tinker's damn about the project."

He ran his fingers through his hair. "Yes, I did. But I didn't say anything about dropping the project."

"You're not backing out of the deal?" She didn't need to turn around to know the mountain predators had encircled her.

"Did you think sleeping with me would persuade me to change my mind?"

Gretchen jerked as if he had slapped her. "Of course not!"

"Then where did you get the idea?"

She opened her mouth to reply, then realized she had nothing to say, and quickly snapped it closed. He hadn't said he loved her! He hadn't mentioned marriage, babies, and happily-ever-afters. Jordon was more than willing to share her bed, but not her life. She had gone that route before, she wouldn't do it again, no matter how much she loved Jordon. The dragons had closed in for their feast. Her sigh held the sound of a heart breaking. "It's getting late, Jordon. I have to get back to the inn." She turned and slowly made her way to his car.

Jordon watched in frustration as she reached the car and got in. He hadn't expected her to walk away. The gutsy mayor of Edelweiss didn't just walk away from an argument. She dug in her heels and fought for what she wanted. So who was that woman sitting in the passenger's seat of his car looking straight ahead? He turned around and probed the landscape. It held no answers.

With a weary sigh he headed toward the car.

Plan A in resolving his stumbling block had failed miserably. He really wished he had a plan B.

Gretchen shivered as Jordon climbed in behind the wheel. He jammed the key into the ignition and started the car. A blast of frigid air poured out of the heater vents. She quickly moved her legs out of the way.

Jordon saw the movement and played with the controls. "Sorry."

"No problem." She glanced out the side window and wished he would hurry up and drive. She wanted to get back to the inn before the threatening flood of tears started to roll.

Jordon drummed his fingers on the top of the steering wheel. "If I back out of the deal now, it would be for purely personal reasons."

She continued to stare at a group of pine trees laden down with huge puffs of snow. His statement didn't require an answer.

Hurt by her lack of response, he cautiously drove back to the inn. Not one word passed between them during the short drive. When she made a move to get out of the car, he gently laid a hand on her thigh. "Dammit, Gretchen, don't put this between us."

"It's always been there."

In frustration he banged his fist against the wheel. "I respect your position not to develop Edelweiss. The least you could do is understand mine."

"Oh, I understand yours, all right. You want the green light to take away productive farmland so that you can cater to the rich. I saw the plans for those condos, Jordon. Not one citizen in Edelweiss could afford the foyer, let alone the entire home."

"Those condos weren't designed for the average person."

"Well, I've got news for you, buddy, that's all Edelweiss has."

Hurt and made irrational by the way things had deteriorated, he snapped, "Why can't you stop being so stubborn and realize all the benefits Edelweiss will gain?"

Gretchen threw open the door and glared at him. "What benefits are you talking about, Jordon? Crowded streets, noisy nightclubs, and higher taxes so that we can afford to give all the services these fine, decent, *rich* inhabitants think is their natural right? In case you haven't noticed, we have only one police officer and one doctor. The firehouse is run by volunteers. How many of your new homeowners will be willing to leave their warm beds in the middle of the night to go fight a fire? Will any of these illustrious homeowners take their precious boats to Eli's Garage, or will there be an influx of new residents to steal the jobs away too?"

She stepped out of the sports car. "Don't you start lecturing me on what will be good for Edelweiss. It's my town. I live here, and you don't. I will have to live daily with your monstrosity, you won't. You'll be back in your fancy high-rise penthouse planning the ruin of another small town." She leaned in closer and snarled, "You might as well head on back there now, bub, because you'll build your stupid condos the day I grow wings and fly."

She slammed the car door, and the noise echoed throughout the valley. She marched through the lobby of the Dragon's Lair, ready to take off anyone's head who so much as wished her a good day. With a trembling finger she stabbed the elevator button and gallantly held back the tears until she reached her apartment.

Jordon pushed his dinner plate away and watched as Gretchen wove her way through the dining room graciously seeing to her guests' every need. Well, there was one guest whose needs weren't being met, and it had only been eight hours since she had stormed out of his car. He had spent the afternoon walking the streets of Edelweiss and trudging up snow-covered hills to get a better perspective of the village and the surrounding area. The only thing he had accomplished was realizing that Gretchen did have some valid points, even if her delivery needed some work, and he missed her unmercifully. He was the one who had forced all the cards onto the table. Now he had to play the hand out.

A pleasant smile touched the corner of his mouth as Gretchen approached his table. "You wanted to see me, Mr. Winters?"

He ignored her cold formality. "I was wondering, Gretchen, if you would consent to share dessert with me? I heard Effie has been busy baking chocolate cakes all day." No harm in trying to raise the ante.

Gretchen felt her mouth start to water. Effie will pay for this treachery later. "I'm sorry, *Mr. Winters*, but I have to work." She refused to answer the silent challenge in his eyes. She knew she should say something about the huge bouquet of orange tiger lilies that had arrived for her at the front desk while she had been out skiing. She didn't. Orange wasn't her favorite color, but the flowers sure did brighten up the lobby. The flowers had surprised her; she hadn't expected their daily arrival to continue. "If you notify the front desk of your departure, I'm sure they will have your bill ready in the morning."

"I'm not going anywhere, Gretchen." He settled back more comfortably into the chair. "I have some unfinished . . . uh . . ."

"Business?" She supplied the word he was looking for.

"No. I believe the word I'm looking for is pleasure." He toyed with a fork. "I've discovered that your enchanting town of Edelweiss holds many hidden pleasures."

Gretchen's eyes narrowed slightly, but she kept the professional smile firmly plastered onto her face. She had a roomful of guests; she didn't have time to play any more games with Jordon. "Enjoy your stay, Mr. Winters." She turned on her heels and headed for the closest table of diners.

Jordon gazed at her graceful curves as she walked away. She could run, but she couldn't hide. Edelweiss wasn't that big. There was no way he was going to allow something as trivial as option clauses and building ordinances to come between them. Somewhere was the answer, and until he found that answer, he wasn't letting Gretchen out of his sight.

His persistence paid off half an hour later when he walked into the lounge and spotted her. She was sitting with a couple of people discussing skiing conditions and some of the advanced slopes. He casually pulled up a chair next to Gretchen, and asked, "Mind if I join you?"

Gretchen ground her back teeth and smiled. "Everyone, this is Jordon Winters. He's been staying at the Dragon's Lair for—what is it, Mr. Winters, a week now?"

He nodded, knowing that she knew exactly how long he had been there.

A flurry of greetings and name sharing passed around the group. He ordered a drink from the waiter and settled in for the haul. Gretchen's good manners would not allow her to leave the gathering soon after he'd arrived.

After he explained to the group that he was a novice at skiing, they left him in peace. He nursed his drink and allowed the conversation to flow over him. Another subject occupied his mind— Gretchen. She was sitting inches away, tantalizing him with her fragrance. The fingers holding her glass were trembling slightly. A knowing smile teased his lips. She wasn't as calm as she appeared.

He surveyed the group and scowled at a golden Adonis named Greg, who dabbled in exports. He was eyeing Gretchen as if she were the after-dinner brandy. Jordon slid his chair closer to Gretchen, causing her glass to quiver. Golden boy only raised an inquisitive brow.

Gretchen felt the heat of Jordon's thigh pressed against her and shivered. If he had moved the chair any closer, he would be sitting in her lap. What did he think he was doing? She totally missed the question Susie asked. "I'm sorry, what was that?" She glared at the piano player, silently casting the blame on him.

"I said, someone told me about a beer festival on Wednesday night. Is that true?"

"Yes, every Wednesday we put on a traditional festival at the local fire hall. There's plenty of food and fun." She jerked as Jordon's fingers played with the fine wisps of hair clinging to her neck. "It's only a couple of blocks away, so the walk's not that bad."

"Walk?"

"Driving to the festival is forbidden because of the beer." She continued to talk, sounding more and more like a travel agent than a gracious hostess. Jordon's fingers were tracing her backbone. Even through the material of her blouse and vest she could detect their sensual heat.

"Gretchen?"

She looked across the table at the attractive man. He was all sunshine and gold. What was his name? Craig? George? It was something like that. "Yes?"

His smile could sell toothpaste. "I asked if you would care to dance."

"I . . ."

"Sorry, pal, but Gretchen has already promised me the first dance." Jordon stood up and held out his hand toward Gretchen.

Gretchen was about to tell him he had surely misunderstood her and to accept Wonder Mouth's offer, when she glanced up and encountered Jordon's piercing gaze. There would be hell to pay if she tried it. Not wanting to cause a scene, she took his hand and followed him onto the microscopic dance floor.

Jordon pulled Gretchen into his arms and held on tight. He had a feeling he was about to dance with a tornado.

Her voice was as sweet as rock candy. "Who's your beneficiary?"

"My mother." He swayed to the music and inhaled her bewitching fragrance.

"She's about to become a very rich woman."

Jordon chuckled and pulled her closer. "What if I apologize for the caveman routine?"

"Does she look good in black?"

He tried the guilty-little-boy look that had al-

ways gotten him an extra cookie. Gretchen didn't
fall for it. "Okay, I'm sorry. I told myself to behave
tonight and not to push you, but that was before
Mr. Steroid asked you to dance. The thought of
you in another man's arms makes my brain twitch
with something that's probably called jealousy."

Gretchen concentrated on counting the beat
of the music. *One, two, three. One, two, three.
One . . .*

"Did I ever tell you how good you feel in my
arms?"

Two, three. One, two . . .

"It's as if we were made for each other." His lips
brushed the hair piled on top of her head. "Remember the night I took every one of those pins
out of your hair?" He felt her fingers lightly caress
the back of his neck.

Three. One, two, three. One . . .

"Remember how we fit together when we make
love?" He gathered her closer and was rewarded
by her astonished "Oh" when his hard arousal
pressed against her middle.

Two, three. One, three, three . . .

"I was this hard the last time we danced."

She kept her eyes closed and willed her body to
stop screaming for the pleasures only he could
give. Only her mind prevented her from taking
Jordon's hand and climbing three flights of stairs
to paradise.

"I was so excited, I almost took you against the
door." His hand curved over her hip as the music
stopped. The piano player was taking his break.
"Now do you understand why I couldn't allow you
to dance with another man?"

"How do you know I would have accepted?" Her
voice came out in little gasps.

He tried to study her expression in the dimly lit room. "Would you?"

Gretchen moved back a step and broke the intimate contact between them. "You should have allowed me the opportunity to answer for myself."

"I respect your independence, Gretchen. It's one of your many wonderful traits I will always encourage." He tried to control the raging jealousy he felt. "But not when it concerns another man."

Too many conflicting emotions assaulted her at once. One minute he's threatening to destroy her town, the next he's hotter than the devil's heart. Within his next breath he's raving like a jealous husband. It was all too much. She needed something Jordon seemed bound and determined not to give her—space. "Listen, Jordon, can we save the lectures for some other time?" She rubbed her temples, trying to ease the pounding there.

He saw the pain in her eyes and felt like a cad. He hadn't meant to hurt her. "Why don't you take a couple of aspirins and go to bed?"

"That's exactly where I'm headed." She started toward the group of guests still gathered around a table groaning from the weight of empty bottles and glasses. Jordon's hand shot out and grabbed her elbow.

"I'll walk you up."

"Do you think I'll get lost?"

"No, but I would sleep better knowing you're safely tucked in for the night." Hell, who was he kidding? He knew he wasn't going to get any sleep; not with Gretchen alone in her bed one floor up.

She glanced over her shoulder at the group. "I was just going to tell them good night." She groaned as Jordon fell in step with her. "Do you realize what they'll think when they see us leave together?"

Everyone's assumptions would have been correct the past three nights. Tonight they couldn't have been farther off the mark.

"Do you care?"

"No, Jordon, I don't care how my guests feel about me. The Dragon's Lair is my only concern."

Even with a pounding headache she can still aim those arrows with amazing accuracy. Jordon managed to be civilized as they bid the group good night and left the lounge. His arm possessively held on to her elbow as they climbed the stairs. He stopped at the bottom of the private stairs to her apartment. With a bow he released the silk cord and allowed Gretchen to step through. A metal click filled the stairwell as he reconnected the cord. He hadn't stepped through.

His finger reached out and he tenderly traced the gentle curve of her cheekbone. "I can't drop the project, Gretchen"—he felt her stiffen—"for the same reason you can't give it the go-ahead. How do I know that you weren't sleeping with me to get your way?"

Gretchen raised her hand. She had never hit a man before in her life, but there was always the first time.

Jordon eyed the raised hand. "Hurts like hell, doesn't it?" The hand slowly lowered. "I was only making a point. I don't think you would sleep with me for any other reason besides wanting to." He waited for her to acknowledge this; she didn't. "If you believe I slept with you for the project, it stands to reason that you would think because you did sleep with me, and I did cancel the project, you bought my surrender with your body."

"I nev—"

"Hush." He placed his finger over her lips. "It's my turn now. You had your say in the car this morning." He removed his hand. "I want you to think about this tonight, that's all. Really give it some serious thought. You're an intelligent woman, Gretchen. You read those reports, now give them a fair chance. Edelweiss is slowly dying, and you know it. Don't block the changes that could save it because of what happened in your past. If the entire project is killed by the town council, I could live with that. But if it's approved, would you be able to accept it?

"I'm giving you fair warning tonight. Starting tomorrow I will let it be known why I'm in town."

Gretchen's legs started to shake. She knew his purpose would be getting around soon; she had been hoping for more time.

"It's all going to be aboveboard from now on. I won't be dealing with the mayor any longer; I can't separate her from you. You don't want the deal, I can understand that, but you have to understand I still want you." He glanced up the steps to the door of her apartment. "I'm going to dream of that door tonight."

Gretchen folded her arms across her chest to hide her body's reaction to his last declaration. She watched as he turned and started to walk away. "Jordon?"

Gray eyes were black with desire as he stopped, turned, and faced her. "Yes?" His whole body was tense and aching.

"I wouldn't have danced with him."

Jordon smiled with understanding. It wasn't much, but it would help ease the ache.

Eight

Gretchen ignored the crowd of men gathered around Jordon and continued to play the accordion with as much gusto as her clumsy fingers could muster. She had managed to botch every song so far. If the looks the rest of the band were sending her expressed their true feelings, she had hit the all-time low in accordion playing. No wonder it was becoming increasingly difficult to find talented players; no one appreciated artistic creativity. So what if she had swung into a resounding rendition of "Roll Out the Barrel" while the other members diligently played "Feelings"? She was running on three hours of restless sleep, and black coffee was flowing through her veins. What did they expect, Mozart?

She tapped her foot and muttered an apology to Otto, the glockenspiel player, as she missed her opening. A crowd of laughing tourists were trying their damnedest to learn a traditional folk dance. Tables were overflowing with food, folks, and fun. The ladies' auxiliary would be making a tidy profit from this evening's activities.

Her fingers missed another note as she watched Claus set an overflowing fondue tray in front of Jordon. The man was trying to bribe Jordon with melted cheese. A small smile teased the corner of her mouth as Jordon acknowledged the bribe but continued in his earnest conversation with Hans and Erik. Hans wasn't a member of the town council, but Erik was. Erik had been shaking his head, counting on his fingers, visibly skeptical in response to everything Jordon had said for the past fifteen minutes. Jordon was going to find that she wasn't the only one with a stubborn streak.

She had lain awake in her lonely bed and recounted everything Jordon had said. He was right in one aspect, Edelweiss was dying. With all its uniqueness and Swiss appeal, death was still knocking at the door. Changes had to happen. As she had finally drifted off into a fitful sleep, she had been wondering why the changes had to be so drastic?

The phone had rung constantly today. Everyone in town wanted to make sure she knew Jordon was after the Beckers' place. She had been treated to a step-by-step accounting of his journey through town. Hans, Claus, two members of the council, and a reporter from the *Edelweiss Review* had stopped by the Dragon's Lair to see where she stood on the issue. She had made her position quite clear with a "no comment."

She had felt like a rat. The town had elected her mayor, and when a critical issue arose, she tossed out a "no comment." Jordon's words from last night kept haunting her. She wasn't blocking the deal because of her past. She was trying to protect Edelweiss from losing its identity. After a series of phone calls to New York she realized that Winters Enterprises wasn't just a little construction company. Jordon employed hundreds of employees, from the simplest gofer on the job site to sophisticated interior designers. She hadn't stepped in front of a man. She stood toe-to-toe with a giant.

As the band wound down the last set with a toe-tapping, whirl-your-partner number, Gretchen studied the giant. He was dressed more casually than the last time he attended the festival. He was so relaxed and into a friendly conversation, he looked like a local. During the two previous band breaks, he had come up to her with a soda in hand. They had stood away from the crowd and silently watched the antics. Greta and Giselle had zeroed in on Wonder Mouth from last night, and Eva, the buxom waitress, was flirting outrageously with a Texan wearing a Stetson. Gretchen had politely thanked Jordon for the drink and had gone back to the band. They had both known this wasn't the time or place to discuss what lay between them. With the close of the evening Gretchen knew the time had come.

Jordon stood up and handed his half-full tankard to the waitress cleaning the table. The tourists and locals had all left, leaving the cleaning to a few hearty souls. The band was packing up, dishwashers were whirling in the kitchen, and a lone janitor was sweeping the floor. The clock had struck midnight, and Edelweiss was rolling up the carpets.

He walked over and took the accordion out of Gretchen's hands. "Same place as last week?"

"Please." She wished the other band members good night and followed Jordon to the closet.

He helped her on with her red cape, zipped up his own coat, and led her outside. The night was clear and cold, not a trace of wind stirred. It was a perfect night for walking. Their breaths were frosty puffs of air. Jordon held her hand and silently followed her to the center of the town. The Dragon's Lair was in the opposite direction, but he wasn't in a hurry for another sleepless night.

Gretchen stopped in front of the bronze statue of William Tell. Someone had brushed the snow off it and the surrounding area. In the dim glow of the streetlights he shone with dignity and pride. She led Jordon over to a wooden bench, brushed off a light coating of flakes, and sat down. "When I was a little girl, I used to sit here and daydream."

Jordon rubbed her gloved hand between his thick gloves and stared at the statue. William Tell looked like a simple peasant with huge muscles cradling a crossbow. "Tell me one of your dreams."

She closed her eyes and dredged up a memory. "Karl Ludwig would ask me out to Lake Conquest, and, as in the legend, we would end up with a dozen kids and live happily ever after in a pink chalet on the edge of town."

"Was Karl your boyfriend?"

"No. Karl was the town's casanova. He never looked twice at me."

Jordon snorted. "I can't believe that."

"It's true." She smiled into the darkness. "He was eighteen, drove a motorcycle all summer and a van with a bed in the back during the winter. I was twelve at the time." She heard Jordon chuckle.

"What's Karl doing nowadays?" He didn't like the idea of casanova on wheels still being in the picture.

"Last I heard, he was selling plots in a pet cemetery in New Brunswick, New Jersey." She settled back on the bench and eyed the statue. "Do you know the legend of William Tell?"

"Sure, he shot an apple off his son's head with a crossbow."

"People always remember that part. No one ever remembers the most important part."

He knew he had just let Gretchen down by the tone of her voice. He tightened his grip on her hand and slid closer on the bench. "Tell me."

"He helped lead the Swiss revolt for independence against the Austrian Hapsburgs in the thirteen-hundreds."

"Ah, so independence runs in your blood."

Gretchen chuckled. "As thick as maple syrup."

Jordon looked at the statue with new respect. "Are you trying to warn me about the independent streak running through the village?"

"You noticed?" She shouldn't have sounded surprised. Jordon was very observant.

"As you said, it's like maple syrup." It was Jordon's turn to chuckle. "Let's say I ended up in a couple of sticky spots today."

Gretchen nodded her head. She could imagine. "Watch out for Claus. The man would sell his mother for a handful of rich tourists."

"I noticed."

"Erik is the strongest member of the council, but he's a skeptic. Jarvis and Luther Emerson could be persuaded if they thought it would keep their children in Edelweiss. Ulrich thinks he's living in the Alps, so forget him. The other two members are anybody's guess. I haven't the slightest idea which way they would go."

Jordon stared dumbfounded at the woman sitting next to him. "Why are you giving me all this information?"

She stared at the statue of the Swiss folk hero. "Independence." Her gaze shifted to the charming stores lining Main Street. This was her town. She had lovingly protected it for the past two years. Maybe it was time for it to face some of life's reality. "It will take a majority vote to override the ordinances. My vote only counts in case of a tie."

"I know."

"I figure it's what Willie here fought for. The independence to cast our own vote. Every member of the council is entitled to make his own decision. That's the responsibility we gave them when we voted them into office." She looked at Jordon. "Give it your best shot."

"Are you serious?"

"You were right last night. The village is dying. If Edelweiss were a cat, I would have to say it's used up eight of its lives. If the council believes this is the best way to go, who am I to stop them?"

Jordon felt humble in her presence. The woman should be president of the United States. He wasn't sure he would be so accommodating if their positions were reversed. "You don't think I'm using you anymore?"

"If I would have thought that, you never would have made it past my front door."

He squeezed both her hands. "Thank you."

"Don't thank me yet. You haven't won anything yet."

"Oh, yes I have." He brushed her chilled lips. "I won your trust, and that's more important than any building." He yanked her to her feet, pulled her into his arms, and swung her around.

Gretchen shrieked as the world whirled by. The man was dangerous. He was lovable, sexy, and extremely dangerous to her heart.

Jordon carefully set her booted feet back on the ground and grinned. "All we have to do is work on you being true to yourself, and then you will be perfect."

To thy own self be true! Had she ever been true to herself? From the time she had barely begun

walking, her mother had strapped skis to her feet.
The first word out of her mouth had been *snow*.
Over half her life had been spent trying to live up
to someone else's dream. At first it hadn't been
that bad—she loved to ski. But as the competition
grew intense, she had to push herself more.
Friends were replaced with downhill runs. All
other winter sports were abandoned in the great
pursuit of faster runs. She had missed ice-
skating, tobogganing, and the sheer fun of a
snowball fight.

It had taken her three years of her life to come to
terms with her parents' death and the realization
that her mother's dreams of an Olympic gold
medal would never be reached. She hadn't the
heart to strap back on the skis and win one.
Maybe it was fear or maybe it had been her first
act of being true to herself. Living with Tom had fit
into her lifestyle but not her heart. Maybe Jordon
was right, she had to start being true to herself.
Having him share her heart, her life, and her bed
for however long he'd be staying in Edelweiss went
against her dreams. She wanted him to love her
back. She wanted the happily-ever-after. "I'm a
long way from perfect, Jordon." She pulled out of
his arms and stepped back. "Are you ready to
head on back?"

A frown pulled at his mouth. "Sure, if you are."
He reached for her hand and held tight as they
made their way back to the inn. Gretchen had
thrown up an emotional block as high as the
Grand Canyon. Why? She had handed him her
trust and took away his heart within the same
gesture.

A gust of wind blew as they made their way up
the stone walk to the inn. Gretchen looked up and
studied the sky. "We're in for snow."

Jordon followed her gaze. He was out of his element. Give him a stretch of white sand and a starry night and he would be able to predict the next day's forecast. Winters in New Hampshire were as unpredictable as Gretchen's moods. "Blizzard?"

"No, only two or three inches sometime before dawn."

He was impressed. "All that from stargazing?"

"No." Gretchen chuckled as they reached the door. "I listened to the forecast before heading to the festival." She reached for the shiny brass knob.

Jordon stopped her and slowly turned her in the dim light. He couldn't read the look in her eyes. He removed his gloves and gently cupped her chilled cheek and pushed the hood back. "You're beautiful."

"My mother would have thanked you." At his look of confusion she explained, "If my mother at thirty-two were standing next to me at this moment, you probably wouldn't be able to tell us apart."

His thumb rubbed her lower lip with a slow, steady motion. "Yes, I would. I'd be able to pick you out of a thousand look-alikes."

Gretchen believed him.

"Why didn't you tell me your mother was Claudia Ruttgers, the world-famous Olympic skier?"

"Ah, the tongues have been busy."

"She was killed in a skiing accident years ago, wasn't she?" He tilted up her chin. "I'm sorry."

"It was half a lifetime ago."

"But it still hurts, doesn't it?" He brushed her lips in a consoling kiss.

"I think it always will." It would be so easy to step into his arms and forget the loneliness. But wasn't he the one who'd been pushing her to be true to herself?

Jordon pulled her into his arms. He tried to think of something comforting to say. He couldn't. He had never lost anyone really close to him. His parents were alive and living it up in a beachfront condo in Florida. His sister was healthy and happily raising her three daughters.

Gretchen felt his arms tighten, and smiled. Words weren't needed. She knew what he hadn't figured out how to put into words. Was that what love was all about? The ability to communicate without words?

Gretchen raised her face. "Thank you, Jordon. You're a very sweet man." *Handsome and sexy too. Oh, by the way I'm in love with you and want to bear your children.* That ought to get his feet moving, right on back to New York.

No one in his life had ever called him sweet, including his own mother. Was she suffering from some type of night blindness and couldn't see what was in front of her? He was a man, a very aroused man. Three nights in her bed and he had became addicted to her. He needed her sweetness to take away the pain. But any woman who called a man "sweet" wasn't planning on spending the night in his bed. The ache would continue. Still, Jordon wasn't a fool. He could wait. "If I ask nicely, will you have dinner with me tomorrow night?"

"You mean tonight?" It was after midnight, and dawn seemed light-years away. It was going to be another long night. She covered a yawn with her hand.

Jordon chuckled. "Come on, sleepyhead, it's time you visited the sandman." He opened the door and ushered her in.

The lobby was empty. "Walt must be on a break," she said, referring to the young man who manned the desk during the night. She headed for the stairs.

Jordon grabbed her elbow and steered her to the elevator. "The condition you're in, the stairs could prove fatal." He pushed the button. The doors immediately opened. "I'll see you *tonight* for dinner." He pressed a kiss to her forehead and gently pushed her into the elevator. "Gretchen"— his hand shot out to block the doors from closing—"I might be 'sweet,' but you taste sweet."

He watched her smile appear as the doors closed. With a weary sigh he turned and headed back across the lobby. The sight of the huge basket of blue carnations made him smile. It was sitting in the place of honor near the dining-hall entrance. Blue hadn't been her favorite color either. The poor florist was getting desperate coming up with a different color every day. Maybe he should send flowers in the color he really thought was Gretchen's favorite color? Nah, she would be disappointed. The last time he had been in her apartment, she had been fussing over every plant like a mother hen, and a pile of plant books was on the coffee table. Gretchen loved receiving his daily surprise.

He walked past the entrance to the lounge, caught the faint clink of glasses, and retraced his steps. The night was stretching endlessly in front of him. He knew two things he wouldn't be having tonight—Gretchen and sleep.

Gretchen glanced at the clock. Six-thirty in the morning and she was up, dressed, and ready to begin her day. Today was the day she was going to make Jordon fall in love with her. For hours last night after Jordon had put her in the elevator, she had paced, yawned, and literally argued out loud with herself. The answers all came down to one thing: She was in love with Jordon. So the best possible thing to happen was for him to fall in love with her. The solution had been so simple, she didn't know why she hadn't thought of it before.

She wasn't unattractive. Jordon, himself, had called her beautiful. Her health was great. Granted, her biological clock had started ticking, but at thirty-two the alarm wasn't ringing yet. She was self-supporting and owned a twenty-four-room inn nestled in the White Mountains of New Hampshire, if one wasn't counting the mortgage Edelweiss National was holding. She could cook when the occasion demanded it, and the thought of cleaning a bathroom didn't send her off into a screaming fit of terror. Their kisses were hotter than dynamite, and when they made love, every celestial dragon shuddered at the explosion. There would be no complaints in that department. She'd make a damn good wife, even if she had to say so herself.

On the down side was the fact she couldn't grow a weed. Two of the violets Jordon had sent looked terminal already, and when the fig tree dropped a leaf she had watered, misted, and jammed a fertilizer stick into its dirt. If a tree could look green around the edges, this one did. The other glaring shortcoming was that she lived hundreds of miles away from him. How was she supposed to run the Dragon's Lair from New York? How was Jordon supposed to head a major corporation from a town that didn't even have a fax machine?

Gretchen reached for the phone. She was getting ahead of herself. First step was to get Jordon to fall in love. They'd worry about the trivial stuff later.

Jordon reached for the ringing phone on the nightstand. Dawn was just seeping into the room. "Yeah?" His voice sounded like sandpaper, and his head was throbbing. What had possessed him to sit in the lounge until closing time drilling the bartender about Gretchen?

"Good morning, Mr. Winters. This is your wake-up call."

He groaned. He hadn't requested a call. Jordon was about to tell the cheerfully impertinent operator what he thought about being wakened at this ungodly hour when a sense of recognition came to him. The voice was familiar, very familiar. "Gretchen?"

"Morning, Jordon."

"What time is it?"

"Six forty-one, and you're going to be late."

He rubbed his eyes and squinted toward the patio door. "For what?"

"Practice."

Why did the pounding in his head echo over her voice? He hadn't the faintest idea what she was talking about. "Practice?"

"Yep. I'll meet you in the dining room in half an hour. Dress warmly and bring your new ski outfit with you."

"We're going skiing?"

"Nope."

"But—"

"Half an hour." She paused for a moment. "Oh, and Jordon?"

"Yes."

"Bring your checkbook."

Jordon stared at the receiver in his hand. Had she said "checkbook"? He pushed himself off the bed, replaced the phone, and refused to hold his head as he made his way into the bathroom. He hated mysterious phone calls first thing in the morning. He hated drinking till two in the morning. He hated waking up to Gretchen's wonderful voice only to realize it was coming across a telephone line.

He turned on both taps full force and stepped in. Gretchen was obviously up to something. She had sounded playful and sexy. He turned down the hot water and punished his aroused body with a blast of cool water. Whatever had put Gretchen into this frolicsome mood had his one-hundred-percent approval. His checkbook was going to show her exactly how much approval.

Gretchen clutched the toboggan and gazed in dismay at Jordon standing next to her. She had wanted him to fall in love, not pay off the mortgage on the Dragon's Lair. He had joined her on time in the dining room. They had shared a marvelous breakfast as she outlined this morning's activity—tobogganing. Every year Edelweiss held a tobogganing competition. The entrants must pay a fee, which was donated to the Special Olympics Fund. The fee was left up to the discretion of each racing team. The winning team got to personally present the check to a representative of the Special Olympics and have their picture taken. The teams usually donated twenty-five or thirty bucks. Gretchen had heard that someone had donated a hundred dollars once. The grand total wasn't a fortune, but every little bit helped. Edelweiss tried to help as many noble causes as possible. The amount of Jordon's check for Monday's race had been mind-boggling. It far surpassed anything Edelweiss had ever contributed before.

Jordon took the toboggan and glanced down the hill. It looked like a pretty straight run to the bottom. At the base of the hill the ground leveled out, and someone had placed bales of hay across the ground. "Explain it again."

"Most toboggans are built for four people, this is only a two-person one. One sits in the front, the other behind him. The person in the back steers by pulling on the cord."

He looked at the length of yellow fiberglass cord attached to the wooden sled in his hands and frowned. "What's the hay for?"

"That's our brake."

Jordon looked over at her to see if she was joking. She wasn't. "Kind of . . . primitive, isn't it?"

"Nah, it's fun." She took the toboggan and set it on the ground. "Do you want to steer or not?" She noticed his indecisive expression as he continued to gaze at the hay bales. "How about I steer the first time and you can try the next run?"

Jordon sat on the sled and pulled up his feet. He felt like a pretzel. "You're the expert."

Gretchen climbed on behind him and wrapped her legs around him. "Ready?"

He liked being a pretzel. "Go!" Nothing happened. He felt Gretchen shaking behind him and glanced over his shoulder at her. She was laughing. "What's so funny?"

"I forgot to mention one little thing."

"What?"

"We have to push off."

Jordon put his hands in the show and pushed hard.

Gretchen hadn't been prepared for his quick movement. Her scream echoed off the mountain and through the valley as they plunged full-speed down the toboggan run on Thunder Mountain. She knew from experience that there were a couple of patches she should try to avoid. She could steer around them expertly; only problem was she was blinded. Jordon's towering bulk sat in front of her, cutting off her view. The only things she could see were Jordon's back and the blue sky.

They hit the first rough spot and vibrated thirty feet down the mountain. Gretchen's back teeth ached. She had been correct last night with the forecast. Two inches of fresh powder covered the packed hill, adding speed to their first run and concealing all the trouble areas.

She heard Jordon's shout and quickly pulled the rope with her left hand. She knew what he saw without being able to see. On the right-hand side of the run was a bump. It had been affectionately nicknamed Speed Bump and left in the run for the sake of adventure. From the top of the hill it was invisible. It made its reputation by sneaking up on unsuspecting people. If they hit it at this rate of speed, they would be airborne. Gretchen definitely didn't want to fly without the aid of an airplane. She put everything she had into pulling the cord.

Jordon saw the cord go tight and felt the toboggan's slight veering. It wasn't enough. They were going to crash. He leaned his weight to the left, heard her warning cry, and hit the bump at the same instant.

He saw blue skies, white snow, and the brown toboggan all at once. His foot had caught in the front curve of the toboggan, and he carried it with him in his frantic roll.

Gretchen went with the momentum and finally came to a stop a couple of yards uphill from Jordon. She quickly got to her feet and half-walked/half-slid her way to him. He didn't look too happy as he spit out a mouthful of snow. Her foot slipped on an icy patch, and she ended up sitting down next to him in the snow. "Are you all right?" She hadn't meant for them to take such a nasty roll. She wanted Jordon to have a great time and to realize how much fun she could be, not suffer internal bleeding.

He dug a handful of snow out of his collar and scowled. He had been having the time of his life until the spill. Next time he would steer. He kept his scowl in place and muttered the two words that were guaranteed to raise every woman's blood pressure: "Woman driver."

Gretchen retaliated by jumping to her feet and hurling a snowball at his chest. "Who was the one who leaned?"

"We were going to plow right over that mountain. Didn't you see it?" He winged a snowball at her feet.

"That wasn't a mountain, it was Speed Bump, and, no, I couldn't see it. Some baboon was blocking my view."

Jordon chuckled as her next snowball grazed his shoulder. "Who was the idiot who built a speed bump in the middle of a toboggan run?"

She ducked as a snowball whizzed by her head. "It isn't a speed bump, it's named Speed Bump." She quickly packed another ball. "It's been here since before I was born."

Jordon made a wild grab for her feet and missed. She laughed and stepped out of his reach. She tried to turn and bolt up the hill. His hand wrapped around her boot and pulled. She tumbled down and slid into his arms.

Jordon rolled her over and positioned himself on top of her to prevent anymore hurling of snowballs. "Did I hear you right?"

Blue eyes innocently blinked. "About Speed Bump?"

"No." He pinned her arms above her head. "I distinctly heard you call me a baboon."

She bit the inside of her cheek. This was the Jordon she wanted to spend the rest of her life with. "You're a very handsome baboon."

He lowered his head and brushed her lips. She tasted like sunshine and snow, crisp, bright, and sinfully tempting. He playfully ran his tongue over the cool moistness. When he felt her lips part in an invitation, he pulled back.

A small whimper of frustration emerged from her mouth. Her smile was pure bewitchery. "You don't kiss like a baboon."

He moved his hips into a more comfortable position. "What do I kiss like?"

She freed one of her hands and pulled his head down. Her reply was whispered against his hungry mouth. "Like my dreams."

Nine

Jordon glanced at Erik and had to admit the man had some very valid questions about the proposed building project. He also had some genuine concerns about Edelweiss's future. Jordon had ventured into the shop to buy a pair of ice skates for tonight. The rentals just hadn't fit his feet right. Gretchen seemed to be born on the ice. He might as well adjust to the fact that he was going to be spending a lot of time outdoors if he wanted to keep up with her.

He signed the charge slip and repocketed his card. "So where's the middle ground, Erik?"

"Good question, Jordon. I wish I knew what to tell you." He placed the box of skates into a bag. "What does Gretchen say?"

"She's being amazingly quiet on the subject."

"Are we talking about the same Gretchen? The one I'm referring to is the mayor of this old town and has an opinion on everything. She has made it her sworn duty to protect and preserve this town."

Jordon chuckled at the accurate description. "That's the one." His tone turned serious as he toyed with the edge of the bag. "We don't discuss business anymore."

Erik raised a brow and straightened his elaborate vest. "Oh?"

"We were coming from opposite ends, and there didn't seem to be a middle ground."

"There's always a middle ground."

"If there is, I haven't found it yet." Jordon looked around at the well-stocked store and frowned. There wasn't another customer in it. "Gretchen is going to back off and allow the town council to do its job and vote."

"If there's a tie, her vote will break it."

"I know."

"What if she halts the building?" Erik asked.

"I can live with that, but could Edelweiss?" He picked up the bag. The conversation had turned too serious and depressing. "There's a middle ground somewhere. There has to be."

Erik pulled at his beard. "The answer is probably right under your nose. It usually is."

Jordon smiled at the simplicity of Erik's logic. Every resident in Edelweiss was straight speaking and reverted everything to its lowest common denominator. "You're probably right, Erik. I'll be seeing you around." He turned, started to walk away, and halted. "Have you ever seen a dragon in the Dragon's Lair?"

"A real dragon?"

"No." Jordon caught Erik's gleam of devilment and knew he was having his leg pulled. "Gretchen said there was only one dragon in the inn that the guests could see if they looked really hard. I've looked everywhere, and the closest thing I could find was Effie standing in the kitchen roaring at some dishwasher for breaking another dish."

"Effie pitching a fit could be classified as a dragon breathing fire. Many a brave man would rather go up against a real dragon than Effie when she's riled."

Jordon silently agreed. The woman did look threatening. "Did you see the dragon or not?"

"Ja, seen it with these very eyes."

"So there is a dragon?" For the past week he began to get the feeling Gretchen had sent him on a wild-goose chase.

"Ja."

"It's not in her apartment, right?"

"No, it's in plain sight for anyone to see who wishes to." Erik pulled his beard again. "I could never fathom why she put it there, though."

"Where?"

Erik's rich laughter filled the shop. "No, Mr. Winters, who is stealing our mayor's heart, I will not tell you."

Jordon lost interest in the dragon. He was more preoccupied with why Erik thought he was stealing the mayor's heart. Their kisses yesterday during tobogganing practice, then later during the barrel-jumping contest and the alpenhorn serenade, had left him hungry and frustrated. Dinner last night had been intimate and romantic. Gretchen had worn a black, clingy dress that had sent his blood pressure rising, along with another part of his body. She had dressed for seduction. Only problem was, no one got seduced. Dinner had been served in a secluded corner of the dining hall. The food had been superb, the conversation exciting, and his imagination had run wild with all the ways he was going to make love to her. The only thing he received was a heated good-night kiss that had melted the soles off his shoes. "You think so?"

Erik grunted. "Do I look like a fool to you?"

Jordon grinned. "No." His step was lighter as he walked out of the sporting-goods shop. Things weren't as bad as he was beginning to think. If the town was noticing the way she was feeling toward him, it wouldn't be that much longer before she would admit it to herself.

He stopped in at the florist, who turned a peculiar shade of white at his entrance, and discussed future bouquets. The poor dear had lost her sense of adventure when he asked her to dye an entire order of carnations, daisies, and mums turquoise.

The morning sun had brightened up the day, and a few tourists were walking through the shops or window shopping. If his plans went accordingly, by next year the sidewalks would be overflowing with prospective customers. He shifted his package to the other arm and headed up the inn's stone walk. Erik's conversation kept playing through his mind. *The answer is probably right under your nose. It usually is.* Jordon stopped in the middle of the walk and stared at the Dragon's Lair. Erik had been right; the answer had been staring him right in the face all this time. He had been too blind to see it before.

Jordon threw open the door of the inn and stared like a man possessed at the young girl behind the reception desk. "Order me a pot of coffee and have lunch sent to my room." He gazed unseeingly around the lobby. "I'm not to be disturbed for any reason. How can I get a fax machine today? Have you seen Gretchen?"

Huge dazed blue eyes stared back at him. The girl hadn't uttered one sound. In exasperation he raised his voice and bellowed, "Gretchen."

Gretchen dropped the clipboard she had been holding and rushed out of the lounge. Her feet skidded on the wooden floor when she saw the look on Jordon's face. Something was wrong. She quickly glanced around and noticed there was no fire, no one was bleeding, and dead bodies weren't littering the lobby. "Jordon, keep your voice down."

Jordon turned at the sound of her voice and swung her up in his arms. "I did it!"

"Did what?" She tried to disengage herself. He was making a spectacle in front of the staff.

"*It*, you know the big *it*."

Gretchen glanced at his face. No white foam was drooling from his mouth; that ruled out rabies. His cheeks were slightly flushed, but he didn't have a fever. The eyes looked overly bright, but clear; there went her drug theory. The man had obviously lost *it*. "Jordon, dear, put me down." Her voice was sweet and steady.

"I will in a minute." He swung her around once more while laughing, and then slowly lowered her back to her feet. "I need your permission for a few changes in my room."

"What's wrong with your room?" It was the first time a guest had complained.

"Nothing's wrong with it. I need some stuff installed, that's all."

Her brow furrowed. "Like what?"

"Another phone line and a fax machine, for starters." He kissed her frown. "I'll pay for everything, don't you worry." Before she could respond, he hurried on, "I won't be able to make dinner, but I'll meet you here at nine so that we can go skating." He kissed the frown again and dashed for the steps. "Oh, and Gretchen, you'd better do something about your girl there, she doesn't look too good." He disappeared up the flight of stairs.

Gretchen turned and studied the dazed expression on Alice's face. The poor girl looked like she was shell-shocked. She couldn't blame her; she felt the same way. Whatever *it* was must surely be important. She had never seen Jordon so excited about something. Well, maybe she had, but it would be unladylike to mention it to poor Alice. "What did he say to you?"

"He wants lunch."

"That's all?"

"No. He wants coffee too. A whole pot, he said."

Gretchen nodded. Jordon was a coffee drinker. "And?"

"Something about the facts and where were you?"

"It's a machine and I'm here." She walked around to the back of the desk. "Why don't you go take a break in the kitchen and while you're there put in Mr. Winters's order."

The blond head nodded as she left her post. Her eyes were trained on the stairs, as if waiting for the lunatic's return, as she darted from the lobby.

Gretchen sighed as the young girl disappeared. What was Jordon up to now? The *it* had to be something to do with the condominiums, but what? He had been so excited. Did he find the answer to their dilemma? Maybe some piece of property in another town? He hadn't seemed to be in a hurry to leave town. In fact he was having another phone line and fax installed in his room. He looked to be staying for quite some time.

Her heart rejoiced with that piece of knowledge, but her mind wanted to know what he was up to. She stared up at the ceiling and tapped her fingers against the counter. She wasn't used to not being the one in control, especially when it came to her town. Wasn't it bad enough she was suffering through long, lonely nights without him? Now she was supposed to put up with him being locked away in his room all day. How in the world was she going to make him see she was the woman he wanted to spend the rest of his life with? Being true to oneself was a royal pain in the rear. In frustration she kicked the desk and grimaced in pain just as two new arrivals walked into the lobby. Her throbbing toe felt broken.

Gretchen paced the lobby, alternating her gaze between the stairs and the clock above the registration desk. Jordon was five minutes late. Jordon was never late. If the kitchen staff hadn't reported picking up empty trays from in front of his door, she would begin to suspect he had left town. No one had seen him since he disappeared up the stairs ten hours ago.

A flurry of commotion and loud grumbling plowing its way down the stairs got her attention. Jordon was shoving one arm into his coat, carrying a box, and had a pair of gloves clutched between his teeth. He looked ruffled, exasperated, and downright adorable.

Jordon hurried over to Gretchen, took the gloves out of his mouth, and kissed her. "Lord, I've missed you."

"I've been here all day."

He took his skates out of the box. "I know, that's what's been driving me nuts." He jammed the empty carton into a wastebasket, draped the skates over his shoulder, and took her hand. "Sorry about being late. Are the others outside?"

"Gunter just got back from taking them to the

lake. We have the sleigh all to ourselves." She seductively smiled as she led the beaming Jordon out of the coatroom and into the backyard. Zelda stood patiently waiting for them. She patted the horse's head and untied the reins from the post. The bewitching smile was still evident as she walked over to Jordon. "If you're a real good boy, I'll let you handle the reins."

Jordon's glance ran down the red cape she had on. He wondered if she was wearing the same skating outfit as last Friday night? Visions of endless legs and a pert bottom heated his blood. His voice was husky as he helped her up onto the sleigh's bench. "I'd rather be handling something else."

Gretchen blushed with pleasure. At least the physical side of their relationship was still simmering. She shoved the reins into his hands. "Handle these for a while."

Jordon chuckled. He clicked his tongue at the horse and gently jiggled the reins. Zelda pranced her way out of the yard and headed for an open field. "Does she know where she's going?"

"Zelda knows the way; you don't even have to control the reins. She can find the lake blindfolded."

Jordon glanced around. They were alone under the night sky. Trees were capped with snow, and the moon wasn't as bright as the last time he shared this ride with her. He placed the reins on the seat next to him and plucked Gretchen from her perch.

Gretchen cried his name in alarm.

He settled her more firmly onto his lap. "Now, what was that about Zelda finding the lake by herself?"

It was a lot more comfortable sitting on his lap

than on the wooden bench. Warmer too. "They have carrots there."

His lips brushed her ear. "Carrots, hmmm . . ."

She encircled his neck with her arms. "Zelda loves carrots and sugar cubes."

Jordon's teeth nipped playfully at her earlobe. "I'll buy her a sugarcane plantation if she takes the long way around."

Gretchen ran her tongue up the outside of his ear. "She doesn't know the long way."

His hand slipped into the cape. Trembling fingers found a long, shapely leg. He lovingly caressed its length, from the top of her boots, over a delicate knee, and up firm thighs. His fingers toyed with the lace trim of her skating panties. His overtaxed mind blew a fuse. How was he supposed to concentrate on solving their problems when she walked around in skirts shorter than her panties? "Are you warm enough?"

Fire raced up her leg at his touch. Warm? She was burning up. She reached for his hand. "No, I seem to have a chill"—she placed his palm against her stomach—"right there."

Heat radiated from his hand as he lowered his head to taste her lips. He plunged his tongue past her lips and into her sweetness. His hold tightened as he felt her response. It was as intense as he remembered. Gretchen Horst belonged in his bed and in his life. And the sooner she realized that, the better off he'd be. His hand skimmed up the soft cashmere sweater and gently cupped a breast.

Gretchen moaned and arched her back. His rich heat had penetrated every pore on her body. A riot of sensations stormed her mind—and bells rang in her ears? Zelda's bells? The ringing suddenly stopped, and she tore her mouth away as an uneasy feeling came over her. Where did the bells go?

Jordon reached for her mouth again. It had felt too wonderful and delicious to give up without a protest. Her lips parted with invitation as the quiet washed over him. He also noticed they weren't moving. He broke the kiss and glanced up.

Elise's hearty laughter filled the air. Her sleigh was loaded down with guests from her bed and breakfast. "This is one of the many ways the Swiss stay warm." Her guests laughed along with her. "It also happens to be the most pleasant way."

Gretchen wished the ground would open up and swallow the other sleigh. She wasn't embarrassed to be caught kissing Jordon, but she was damn annoyed at the interruption. Where was a good fire-breathing dragon when you needed one? "Greenpeace wholeheartedly endorses kisses as an alternative way of keeping warm."

Jordon chuckled. His spitfire wasn't going to shrink in terror about being caught kissing her. His arms tightened protectively around her.

Elise laughed again and yanked on her reins. "*Ja,* they would, little one." Her sleigh started down the path, and Gretchen obligingly waved back to the guests. Elise's rapid-fire German filled the air.

Gretchen beamed at the older woman. "One can live in hope."

"What did she say?"

A blush swept up her cheeks as she climbed off Jordon's lap and settled back onto the bench. She couldn't tell him what Elise had said, not because it was bad, but because of her response. How could she tell him that Elise had said, "Beware, kissing also leads to little bundles of joy"?

"It was nothing." Gretchen reached for the reins and clicked Zelda back into motion.

Jordon couldn't read her expression in the darkness. Whatever Elise had said wasn't nothing. By Gretchen's response she had wanted whatever Elise had said. He made a mental note to find Elise and wheedle the information from her.

The horse got them to the lake. "She did know the way," he said.

Gretchen allowed Zelda to set the pace for the shelter. "I told you she would." They came out of the trees and into the opening. "Looks crowded tonight."

"Why isn't there night skiing?"

"There is. Every Saturday night we have a candlelight run."

Jordon looked at the lake and the crowd. Candlelight skiing sounded intimate and romantic. "Why don't you go? Lord knows you attend everything else in this town, from the barrel-jumping competition to the alpenhorn serenade."

"Didn't you enjoy them?"

He jumped from the seat and turned to help Gretchen down. "You know I did." He threw the reins over the post and got Zelda her carrot. "I still think the barrel jumpers were either high or drunk. No sane man would willingly jump a group of barrels on ice skates." He held her hand as they walked toward an empty bench. "I have an idea. Why don't you hold the barrel-jumping contest after one of your beer festivals? You would have a lot more entrants."

"And a lot more accidents." She shuddered to think of the mayhem mixing beer and ice skates could cause. "What about the alpenhorns?" It was one of her favorite and one of her least-favorite events. The low, rough timbre the instruments produced and the simple melodies played on them combined to create an unparalled haunting experience. Sixteen years ago, as they lowered the bodies of her parents into the frozen ground, Edelweiss paid its final and most distinguished honor to them by having the alpenhorns echo off the mountains. Their sound had seemed to last forever. To this day every time she heard an alpenhorn, tears formed in her eyes. Most of the residents felt the same way as they remembered a lost loved one.

"They were"—he paused looking for the right word—"moving. I'm not sure if that's the correct word, but it's the best I can do. It was almost eerie, like something should be happening. I kept waiting for something to appear."

"Like dragons returning from the hunt."

Jordon stopped lacing up his skates and studied her bent head. Was she serious? "I wouldn't have been surprised if one of your mythical beasts had soared across the heavens."

Gretchen smiled. He might not have been surprised, but she would have had a coronary.

He saw her fleeting smile. Why would she be smiling now, when during the serenade he would have sworn she had tears in her eyes? Half the people standing around the base of Thunder Mountain had had that same look. He had seen veterans get that look as the flag passed them during a Memorial Day parade. "You still never answered the original question."

"What was it?" She got to her feet and unbuttoned the cape.

"About why you don't ski in the candlelight procession?"

"That's simple." She placed the coat on the back of the bench and grinned at Jordon's astonished look. Her outfit was pure white, from her fluffy, rub-your-hands-all-over-me sweater to the short skirt that showed every lacy ruffle on her panties. She turned to the ice and pushed off. "It's too slow for me."

Jordon stood up in a daze to follow his snow angel. She was all light and gorgeous. Could a person become blind from seeing an angel? He took two shaky steps onto the ice and ended up on his butt.

Gretchen quickly circled back. "Are you hurt?"

He stood up with her help and dusted off his rear. "Only my dignity."

She eyed the bruised area. Facing him, she started to weave her way backward through the crowd. "If I do say so myself, Mr. Winters, you do have one of the finest-looking dignities this town has ever seen."

Jordon growled, felt his skates start to slide out from under him again, and instinctively grabbed the lady next to him. They both hit the ice with a resounding thud. A curse escaped his lips. Not only was his dignity bruised, but his respectability was bent, and he might not be able to use his good intentions ever again.

Gretchen stepped over the empty lunch tray and knocked on Jordon's door. She was breaking her promise to him that he wouldn't be disturbed. Things had gotten out of hand. She hadn't seen him in two days. When an employee from the phone company showed up first thing on Saturday morning, she was impressed. The boxes that had been delivered later raised a few questions, but she had contained her curiosity. Sunday produced three empty meal trays, but no Jordon. It was only Monday afternoon, and she had reached the end of her rope. Her lobby was in shambles, her desk clerk had threatened to quit, and Effie had just refused to send up another pot of coffee until Mr. Winters proved he was alive. The overnight packages started to arrive at seven-thirty that morning. At last count there had been twenty-six different packages from eight different carriers. The poor desk clerk had signed her life away this morning.

Now, to top off her morning two men and a woman were standing in her lobby with suitcases and bulging briefcases. They had waltzed right in and stated they were from Winters Enterprises and that they were expected. The last thing she had been expecting was an invasion from Winters Enterprises.

Gretchen had been very proud of the way she had held her temper and politely sat the white shirts in the lobby while she went to confront Papa Bear in his den.

Jordon opened the door and squinted. "Gretchen?"

She was shocked by his appearance. He hadn't shaved since Friday night, and by the looks of his wrinkled clothes she wasn't sure when he had changed last. "Lord, Jordon, can't you see?"

He opened the door wider. "Eyestrain."

"Don't you wear glasses?"

"I have been, but after so many hours they don't help." He leaned against the door in a friendly gesture but didn't invite her in. "Can I help you?"

Gretchen folded her arms across her chest. "There are three people downstairs who claim to be from Winter Enterprises. They said they were expected."

"Great. Why didn't you send them up?"

"I wasn't expecting them."

Jordon frowned at her harsh tone, but then understanding dawned. "I forgot to tell you."

"Bingo."

"Lord, I'm sorry, Gretchen. It completely slipped my mind. I'm so used to working with an assistant who follows up on the small details that I forget."

"Small details?" Gretchen's voice was hurt.

Jordon stepped out of the room and wrapped his arms around her. "I didn't mean it that way, honey." His hands lightly caressed her back. She felt so damn good in his arms. "The Dragon's Lair is very important to me"—he tipped up her chin so that he could see her face—"but not as important as you." His lips slanted across her mouth. He took the kiss that had been haunting what little sleep he had been getting.

Gretchen rose to her toes and put the past three days' worth of frustration into the kiss. Jordon's rough jaw scraped her cheek, and she flinched.

The kiss was broken immediately by Jordon. He glanced at the red mark on her cheek and raised his hand to her jaw. A muffled curse tumbled off his lips as he tenderly rubbed the red blotch on her face. "I'm sorry, Gretchen." With a weary sigh he slumped against the wall. "I haven't been very good company lately, have I?"

"In what way?"

"I'm sure by now I've missed six different events."

"You'll miss the most important one if you're not downstairs in half an hour." She couldn't help but notice his confused look. "Remember, this afternoon is the toboggan races."

"Lord, I almost forgot." He glanced desperately around the hall. Time hadn't come a-creeping, it came roaring through. "Is it really this afternoon?"

"Yes. Don't you want to do it?" Her voice quivered with disappointment.

"Of course I do. It's just with the council calling a meeting for Thursday night I don't have a whole lot of time."

"For what? I thought everything was ready for a formal presentation."

Jordon closed his eyes and leaned his head against the wall. "Oh, Gretchen, if only you knew."

"Knew what?"

"*It.* I told you, I figured *it* out."

She tenderly gazed at the man she loved. He looked exhausted and in dire need of some fresh air. "Why don't you go get ready for the race? I'll meet you downstairs in ten minutes."

"No can do. I need the whole half an hour to orient my staff."

She knew how hard he had been working; the evidence was etched into his face. He was desperately working on their problem, and he didn't have too many days left to convince them of the advantages and virtues of his condominiums.

"Jordon, Howard Hughes went out more often than you."

He chuckled. "How about if I meet you in the lobby in twenty minutes? I promise to try my damnedest to win the race, and I will personally treat you to a wonderful dinner and moonlight stroll."

Amused, she said, "It's in the teens outside."

"Who said it will be a long stroll?"

Gretchen chuckled. "Okay, but what should I do with your staff?"

His face was sheepish. "Do you have three vacant rooms?"

"You're in luck, Winters." She picked up the empty tray and started down the hall. "Be in the lobby within twenty minutes, or I will personally drag you kicking and screaming into the fresh air and sunshine."

Jordon growled his frustration as Gretchen disappeared down the stairs. He would love to spend the entire day with her playing in the snow, but he only had three days left to wrap up the most important presentation of his life. Because what he would be presenting to the council just might be his life.

Ten

Gretchen raised her champagne glass and lightly tapped his. "I'll drink to that, Jordon, but I don't see how you can claim we're the best tobogganing team in America. We came in sixth."

"The judges obviously don't know the best when they see it."

Her soft laughter turned a couple of heads in the dining room. She admired the handsome man sitting across from her. Jordon looked just as devastating in a suit as he did bundled up in his ski outfit. His cheeks still held the color from this afternoon's activities. "All those timers couldn't have been wrong."

"Timers can be bought." It still upset him that they hadn't won. Gretchen deserved better. If only he had had the time to practice more. He was the newcomer to this crazy sport of kamikazing down the side of a mountain, Gretchen was the pro.

"You don't buy timers, Jordon. Especially timers in a race where the participants win absolutely nothing."

Jordon smiled tenderly at the woman who had captured his heart. She had ridden the toboggan like a storm trooper, once even yelling, "Take no prisoners," as they plunged down the side of the mountain. With a little practice on his part they could take first place. "Next year we'll win."

Gretchen's hand, holding the glass, froze in midair. *Next year?* Had he really said that? What was he planning to do, come back for a vacation? Or was he confident that the condominiums would be built and that he could oversee their construction? Next year was three hundred and sixty-five days away. She didn't care about then— she wanted now, today, and tonight. The nights had been too lonely. She had missed Jordon's touch. Being true to oneself shouldn't have to be such torture. But even if love didn't bloom on his side, she would still know that whatever they had shared was special. The daily delivery of flowers was the most romantic thing that had ever happened to her. "Thank you for the flowers. They are lovely, as usual."

His eyes twinkled with amusement. "Silver, right?"

The arrangement of dyed asters, mums, and baby's breath was sitting on her kitchen counter. "I'm afraid silver isn't my favorite color either."

"Mrs. Oberholtzer won't be pleased with that piece of news."

"Should I tell you what my favorite color is?" Some inner voice pleaded with her not to. She was delighted with the daily bombardment of flowers. The plants were another story, which reminded her to question Effie about the huge pink begonia that was delivered yesterday; it looked piqued already.

Jordon slowly shook his head. "No, it's a challenge." His gaze locked with hers. "I love a good challenge." He had already guessed what her favorite color was; he was waiting for the right moment to personally present her with the bouquet. Edelweiss was a challenge he was pretty sure he had figured out. It was being worked on around the clock by him and every available employee he had.

Gretchen was the most important challenge of his life. He wanted her love. Since he had never wanted anyone's love before, he was stuck with the dilemma of how to achieve this honor. The flowers had seemed like a good beginning. If he could revitalize Edelweiss and prove there was a middle ground on every issue, he might further his goal. But what he truly needed was a humdinger of a finish. He needed to show Gretchen how he really felt.

Gretchen was the first one to break the eye contact. The intense emotions flaring in his eyes had unnerved her. She couldn't envision what he was thinking, but whatever it was, she wanted to be part of it. She glanced down at their empty plates. Laughter teased her lips. She couldn't remember what she had had for dinner. "It's a little chilly outside for a walk."

Jordon smiled. Only Gretchen would consider eight degrees chilly. She was definitely not dressed for a brisk walk. Three-inch burgundy heels matched her dress. No one could call the dress revealing with its high neck, long sleeves, and a hem that hid her knees from view. But when she poured her delectable curves into the fabric, magic happened. A gold chain and matching earrings were her only jewelry. She looked sophisticated, gorgeous, and sexy. "We wouldn't want to tempt frostbite."

The dining room suddenly became too crowded. She wanted to be alone with him. Time was running out. "Would you like to have dessert up at my place?"

Jordon's gaze turned hot as it slowly left her face to stop on the gentle swell of her breasts. He knew what she was asking. It was written in her eyes. If they went upstairs, he wouldn't be down before morning. Lord, how he wanted to say *yes*. His body was screaming in agony. He reached out and held one of her hands. A sad smile touched his mouth as her fingers trembled within his grasp. "I can't."

Gretchen closed her eyes as disappointment washed over her. She quickly reopened them and smiled brilliantly. "That's okay, all I had was some ice cream anyway."

"Gretchen." His control nearly broke at her brave front. What had he ever done in his life to deserve her? "I didn't say I didn't want to, I said I couldn't."

"Why?"

"One of my rules in business is never to ask my employees to do something I won't do."

Gretchen toyed with the champagne glass with her free hand. "They're upstairs working, aren't they?"

"Yes." He rubbed her wrist with his thumb. "So are about one hundred other people in New York."

"Around the clock?"

"They know the deadline—Thursday at six-thirty."

She chewed on her lower lip. "I thought you had everything ready. Remember, I'm the one who saw it all. I don't understand what's going on, Jordon."

"I know you don't." He squeezed her hand. "I'm sorry about that, but I can't explain it all yet.

There are too many loose ends. On Thursday everything will become clear." His voice was somber as he asked a very important question. "Can you trust me till then?"

Gretchen didn't hesitate. "Yes." She returned his squeeze and smiled. "I didn't promise I would agree with you. I haven't the foggiest idea what you are up to, but I trust you're doing something you think is fair."

"Thank you." He glanced around the full dining hall and groaned. He wanted to reach over the table and kiss her.

She followed his gaze and felt his frustration. The Dragon's Lair wasn't known for its seclusion and privacy. It tended to be friendly and open. If he could wait until Thursday, so could she. Who knows, maybe Thursday was the day for miracles. "How about if I walk you out to the lobby and say good night? I'm sure you must have plenty to do."

Jordon rose and came around to her side of the table and held her chair. "You won't be sorry, Gretchen. It's all going to work out."

She smiled and preceded him from the room. "To show my good faith in you, I'll send up a pot of coffee and a tray loaded with goodies on the house." She stopped at the bottom of the stairs.

Jordon tucked a wisp of her hair back into the braid streaming down her back. "We would appreciate it." He tenderly cupped her cheek and, not caring who was in the lobby, he kissed her.

Gretchen responded to his touch by melting into his arms. Disappointment surged through her as he broke the kiss and put a few inches between them.

He tenderly traced the moisture on her lower lip. "I'll be in touch with you tomorrow." He disappeared up the stairs.

Gretchen turned and smiled pleasantly at the young man behind the registration desk. He looked like a fish with his eyes bulging and his mouth hanging open. One would think he'd never witnessed a man kissing a woman before.

Gretchen entered her apartment the following afternoon and knew someone was there. More curious than afraid, she silently walked through the living room, peeked into the kitchen, and headed down the hall. Her footsteps faltered when she looked into her bedroom. Jordon was sprawled facedown across her bed, fully dressed, and fast asleep.

She had been going crazy for the last half hour looking for him. Effie said he had wandered into the kitchen earlier looking for her and stealing a handful of cookies. She had checked in his room, only to find three other people looking hassled, exhausted, and grumpy, busily pouring over papers, talking on the phone, or yanking sheets out of the fax machine. Jordon wasn't there, and by their attitude she gathered they were extremely happy about it.

She had searched the inn but came up empty-handed. To think, all this time he had been in her bed. She walked over to the bed and stared down. Even in sleep, lines of exhaustion were still etched into his face. His hair was tousled and his clothes were wrinkled. Since it was only three o'clock she would lay money on the fact he hadn't gone to bed all night. Whatever he was working on was going to kill him, if she didn't do the honors first.

She bent over and slipped his shoes from his feet. His clothes would have to stay. There was no way she could strip him without waking him up.

She lovingly brushed a wayward curl off his fore-head and placed a gentle kiss on his lips. He seemed to smile in his sleep. She quietly closed the drapes against the bright afternoon light and draped a blanket over him. After unplugging the phone, she closed the bedroom door and left the apartment. He should sleep for hours.

Jordon awoke disoriented and warm. The last thing he remembered was looking for Gretchen. He had taken the elevator up to her apartment and found her door unlocked, again. Her bed had looked so soft and inviting that he had lain down while he thought about where else she might be.

He squinted at the digital clock and jumped off the bed. It was nine o'clock. He had slept for six hours! Blankets tangled around his feet as he glanced around the dark room. Gretchen must have covered him. He stumbled into the bathroom and flicked on the light. He stared around in wonder. A pair of his pants and shirt were hanging from the towel rack, and his shaving stuff was placed on the counter along with fresh underwear and socks. Gretchen had obviously wanted him to feel at home. With a flick of his wrist he turned on the shower and stepped in.

Gretchen heard the bathroom shower running and heated up dinner. She nervously stirred the sauce and prayed she would at least have a chance to feed him before he found out what she had done. Weren't men with full stomachs easier to manage?

She had just finished setting the table when he walked into the kitchen. His hair was damp, and he looked rested, freshly shaven, and incredibly sexy. "I hope you like spaghetti."

"Is that what smells so good?" He came up behind her and wrapped his arms around her. His nose nuzzled her neck. "I thought it was you."

She turned her face and brushed her lips across his. "Sweet talker." She playfully pushed him away. "Carry the noodles over for me, please."

Jordon picked up the dish, but not before getting the kiss he wanted.

The conversation during dinner was so stilted that Jordon finally laid down his fork. "Are you upset because I slept in your bed?"

"No."

"Mad at me for letting myself in without your permission?"

"Of course not."

"Then what's the problem? You're acting mighty strange." This was not his normal snow angel sitting across from him. This woman jumped at every question and seemed to be sitting on a hot plate.

"I have one of Effie's cakes for dessert."

Jordon frowned. Something was wrong. "You know I have to get back downstairs."

"To join the others who are busily working, right?"

"Yeah." He didn't like the way she phrased that.

Gretchen took a deep breath and blurted out the truth. "They're not there."

"What do you mean, they're not there?"

"They're downstairs in the dining room enjoying a decent meal, then they are either to go enjoy the lounge or go to bed."

"They left the project?" He had promised all three employees bonuses only a top-notch executive could dream about for completing the project on time.

Gretchen turned bright red and shifted in her chair. "You did give them your permission."

His eyes narrowed with a suspicious thought. "I did?"

She couldn't meet his gaze. What she had done had been dishonest. "They were very appreciative too. Brad said you were the best."

Jordon frowned.

"You also gave the order to be back on the job by six and that breakfast will be served then."

Jordon tried to keep his stern expression. He couldn't. He threw back his head and laughed. The little minx had pulled another one over him. First she made him fall in love and now she was giving orders in his name. How was he going to control her? Hell, who wanted to control her? He was more happy with her the way she was, he wouldn't change one thing about her. He continued to laugh as he picked her up and swung her around.

Gretchen was taken aback by his laughter. No man liked to have his authority threatened. But she glanced at his face and realized he was happy. "You're not mad?"

"I'm mad as hell, you little minx. I'm tempted to take you either over my knee or to bed." He swung her around again. "Which should it be?"

She pretended to consider her options.

He cradled her against his chest. "Time's up. I guess I get to choose." He started down the hall toward the bedroom.

"Jordon, wait!"

He stopped.

"I have to clear off the table and put away food."

"You stopped me for that, woman?" He continued on his way.

Gretchen chuckled. Given a choice between congealed tomato sauce and Jordon, he would win hands down every time. This was definitely not the time to prove to Jordon she was a good housekeeper.

Jordon felt the soft swell of her breasts against his chest and groaned. "Lord, woman, stop that laughing or I can't be held accountable for my actions."

Her teeth lightly nipped at his earlobe. "Quick, there's a door on your left."

Jordon marched into her room and lowered her onto the center of the bed.

He started to unbutton his shirt as he gazed at her. She looked sexy and alluring in a pair of faded jeans and an oversized sweatshirt. Her feet were bare and her toenails were painted fire-engine red. Her hair was spread out like a blanket of shimmering gold.

Propped up on her elbows, Gretchen admired the view. Jordon was doing a very slow striptease for her enjoyment. And, boy, was she enjoying it. When he lowered the zipper on his pants, his arousal came into view. Jordon Winters wanted her. There was no denying the obvious.

As he kicked his pants aside and pulled off his socks, she knelt on the bed and pulled the sweatshirt over her head.

Jordon gulped in a breath. She hadn't been wearing a bra, and her breasts were creamy mounds tipped with dusty-pink nipples pouting for his attention. Fascinated, he watched as Gretchen slowly undressed. He had made love to this woman before, but she had never undressed for him. Their lovemaking had been frantic and wild. Tonight he wanted to go slow and show her the magic. Make her see, feel, and taste the magic.

Her jeans landed on the floor. She was naked except for a scrap of red silk. Her eyes questioned him as she toyed with the band of the panties. He forced one word past his dry lips. "Please."

Gretchen faintly smiled and slid the silk down her thighs, past her calves, and over the side of the bed. She pushed the red satin comforter onto the floor with her foot and lay down on the black sheets. Tonight wasn't a night for covers. She wanted the lights on and her eyes wide open. With fingers that trembled with anticipation, she held out her hand.

Jordon tenderly kissed each quivering finger and joined her on the bed. His gray eyes turned nearly black with desire as her free hand buried itself in the thick mat on his chest. He released her fingers and seized her mouth.

She felt the desire clear down to her toes. A warm sensation pulsed in her abdomen, and moist liquid heat gathered at the junction of her thighs, waiting for him. Her toes curled in anticipation. His name tumbled from her lips onto his. "Jordon."

He tasted his name with his tongue. It tasted like Gretchen. He liked that. He swept his tongue into her mouth and gently cupped a soft breast. Her purr of pleasure rolled over his feverish body. He released her mouth and kissed an ardent path to the rigid peak nudging his palm.

Gretchen arched her back and held Jordon's head closer as his teeth lightly grazed her nipple. Her thighs parted instinctively and her hips tilted upward. His warm tongue laved the nub with moistness. She shivered as he gently blew across the damp area.

Jordon pulled back and gazed at her. "You like that?"

She pulled his head down to the other peak. "Please."

"I could never refuse when you say it that way." He duplicated the procedure on the firm nipple. Her shudder sent another blast of desire ripping through his body. "I could do this all night."

Gretchen weakly chuckled. She was barely holding on to her self-control. "No, you can't."

Jordon raised his head to accept the challenge and saw her strained look. She was already on the brink. "Oh, love."

She closed her eyes and savored that word. He had called her *love*. Strong masculine fingers skimmed down her stomach to tangle in the golden triangle of curls above her womanhood. Her breath caught as his lips fastened on the sensitive nub while he dipped a finger into her heat.

"So ready." His voice held awe as he changed position.

Her hips lifted off the bed as his hips nuzzled the inside of her thighs. Rough hair teased satin-smooth skin. "Jordon"—her voice was a whimper—"please."

Jordon captured the sweet sound of her voice with his mouth and thrust. Heated flesh wrapped around him. He ran his tongue over the inside of her lower lip; the textures were the same—moist, slick, and incredibly warm.

"Jordon" was muffled against his lips.

He released her and pulled out to the very edge of sanity.

Gretchen felt his retreat and wrapped her graceful legs around his hips. She didn't want him to leave her. Not ever. She gazed up into his flushed face and studied the tension there. Her hand reached up and cupped his jaw. With tears gathering in her eyes, she whispered the words she prayed he would welcome. "I love you."

Jordon's wishes had been answered. She loved him. He kissed the palm of her hand, her eyelids, and the end of her nose. "Tell me I'm not dreaming."

She wiggled her hips and smiled as sweat broke out across his brow. "Does that feel like you're dreaming?"

Jordon bit his lip as she beckoned him deeper. "No," he answered. Unable to resist the paradise that awaited him, he threw back his head and sank into heaven.

Gretchen tightened her thighs around him and matched his every movement.

Her soft cry of ecstasy was joined with his harsh cry of release.

Jordon carefully moved his arm out from under Gretchen. In her sleep she frowned and tried to find his warmth again. He silently slipped out of bed and padded naked through her apartment, making sure the doors were locked. He smiled at the plates still on the table. He would gladly clean it up in the morning. He turned off the lights, set the alarm, and pulled the comforter back up on the bed, tenderly tucking it around Gretchen and himself.

In the darkness he glanced at the dragon carved into the headboard. Most of the lines and color were veiled by the night, but the topaz eyes still blazed as if they were alive with a hidden fire. He reached up and stroked the dragon. "Thank you for guarding her throughout the years, Chung."

Eleven

Gretchen entered the packed firehouse hall and groaned. It seemed that every resident of Edelweiss had come to hear Jordon's official proposal. It was only natural, since the final decision would affect everyone, but it still made her anxious. What if Jordon's master plan failed. The whole town would witness his defeat.

She slowly made her way toward the front of the hall, where the council was seated. People greeted her and asked questions. She smiled politely and told everyone to save their questions for later. All concerns would be addressed before the vote was taken. It looked as if it was going to be the longest meeting on record.

She spotted Jordon and his three assistants huddled around a small table. Four overflowing briefcases lay open before them. As her glance settled on Jordon, he looked up. Their eyes met and held. Secrets, meanings, and dreams flashed between them. Jordon smiled a dazzling smile before turning back to the business at hand. Ever since Monday night he had followed more reasonable hours and had spent every night in her bed. He might not be getting more sleep, but the exercise had put an extra spark in his eyes.

Gretchen took a deep breath to settle the mammoth butterflies in her stomach and made her way to her usual seat. The mayor always sat at the same table as the council and voted at the same time. Her ballot would be read if, and only if, there was a tie. Gretchen prayed with all her might there wouldn't be a tie.

Erik thumped his gavel, and the room became quiet. After the usual speech that included calling the meeting to order and reading the minutes from the last meeting, he announced it was time for new business. Erik cleared his throat. "Since we have a very important matter to vote on tonight, the council has decided that the only issue we will discuss will be the Winters Enterprises proposal." He glanced around the packed hall and saw no objections. "At this time I would like to turn the mike over to Mr. Jordon Winters, president and owner of Winters Enterprises. Please save all your questions until after his presentation. Mr. Winters has graciously consented to address all fears, concerns, and questions from the floor."

Gretchen cringed as only a light scattering of applause was given to Jordon. Her town was on the defensive. She glanced at Jordon and flushed deep pink when he met her gaze and winked. The man was incorrigible.

Jordon took the mike and spoke to the packed hall. "First, I would like to thank you all for coming. It shows me that the residents of Edelweiss care about their town. It also tells me I made the right decision on choosing Edelweiss. I must confess that I had originally come here thinking that I could waltz into town and have the residents, the town council, and the mayor eating out of my hand within a week." He looked contrite. "You have my humblest apology for that.

"I would like to take a few moments of your time and tell you about the initial proposal I had brought with me."

Gretchen studied the faces of the council as Jordon went into great detail about the condominiums. The facts and figures were the same ones she had read and reread. She already knew which way her vote was going. By the looks on the council's faces and those of a vast majority of the residents, Jordon was doomed to failure. Edelweiss was not ready to take such a drastic step.

She had no idea what Jordon had up his sleeve, but whatever it was, it had better be good. Their lovemaking last night had been slow and sweet. The only thing missing had been those magic words *I love you* from Jordon. She wanted those words. She wanted forever. He had left her bed some time before dawn to join the others and mastermind their presentation. So far she hadn't heard anything new.

"I would like it to be noted that I am not submitting that proposal to the council to vote on." Jordon smiled as silence filled the hall and the council's mouths fell open. Even Gretchen looked confused. "After talking to your mayor and some members of the council, I came to realize they were right. Edelweiss is a unique town. It merits something better than a bunch of flashy high-rise condos. It deserves something unique."

He walked over to an easel holding a covered picture. "Please keep in mind that my staff and I had less than a week to pull this presentation together. All of the artwork is still in the primary stages. Every one of you will agree, if you look deep into your heart, that Edelweiss is slowly dying. Your children grow up here in peaceful serenity only to leave because Edelweiss can't support them." A murmur of agreement whispered through the hall. "Industry will never be the savior of your town. You are too remote. The cost of shipping in raw materials would kill you. From the surveys I have studied, you already use all the available land for agriculture and ranching. That leaves you with what you have now, service." He smiled at the low grumbling. "Edelweiss is a service town, and there isn't very much you can do about it.

"It's also your best asset." That got some raised eyebrows. "What you need is more tourists to shop in your stores, ski on your slopes, and climb your mountains. You will need these tourists to come all year long, not just for a few months during the winter. You will also need someplace for those tourists to stay. The Dragon's Lair and your assorted bed and breakfasts can't accommodate the amount of tourists required to keep this town prospering."

Gretchen frowned but couldn't argue the point. The Dragon's Lair had only twenty-four guest rooms.

"What I'm proposing isn't new to this country, but it will be the first for Winters Enterprises. It's called a hotel, but in reality it is a condominium/hotel. People buy the condominium units, but when they are not in use, they will be rented out. The general idea behind this is that instead of having condos that are occupied, say, only a couple of weeks out of the year, you will have, hopefully, constant occupation.

"The hotel will have the same types of facilities as my proposed condominiums did. When you're rich enough to buy a condo for just a few weeks a year, you expect certain amenities. There will still be the golf course, tennis courts, and swimming pools."

His hand toyed with the picture cover while one of his assistants stood up ready to hand out smaller prints to the council. "The crowning achievement of this proposal is that the hotel will fit perfectly into your unique town. No one coming to Edelweiss for the first time will guess that the hotel wasn't part of the original town." He pulled the cover off and allowed the residents their first glimpse of Hotel Edelweiss.

Gretchen stared at the colored drawing in her hand and blinked back the tears. Jordon had done it. He had designed a hotel that not only delivered what he'd said it would, it was breathtaking. It rose five stories tall with steep roofs and gabled windows. Balconies complete with flower boxes bursting with color surrounded every floor. It was a simple creamy yellow and brown, but the landscaping brought it to life. Shadow Mountain overlooked it, huge pine trees converged around it, and acres of blooming gardens gave the hotel just the right touch. Hotel Edelweiss was perfect.

Jordon was going to get the council's approval. She should be ecstatic, but she wasn't. She was happy that he was sensitive enough to understand Edelweiss's uniqueness, but what about them? He hadn't said he loved her, and to add to the misery her flowers didn't arrive today.

Jordon glanced in Gretchen's direction as he continued to pitch his project, but he still couldn't read her expression. He wished she would look up so that he could see her face better. "Winters

Enterprises will be the first to admit to not being an expert on Swiss tradition, so I am personally asking for your help in that department. Winters Enterprises is giving you a chance to keep Edelweiss's uniqueness and to help your town." He looked over at Gretchen and couldn't tell if she was even listening.

Gretchen's red fingernail traced a cluster of pink flowers on the drawing. Why did the flowers stop? Maybe Mrs. Oberholtzer was running late on the deliveries? Maybe Jordon had given up trying to guess her favorite color? Her wandering thoughts vanished as Jordon's words penetrated her musing.

"Since this is the first Winters Enterprises undertaking of a hotel/condominium, I will be personally overseeing the construction."

Gretchen looked up. Her blue eyes collided with his emotion-packed gray ones.

"Not only will I be overseeing the construction of Hotel Edelweiss, but I will be staying on to manage it."

Gretchen's eyes widened in shock. He will be staying! Love radiated in her smile.

Jordon gazed at her glowing face and winked. He started to field the questions coming from the residents and the council. The mayor was conspicuously quiet.

Two hours later he couldn't take another question. The council seemed to be in agreement to allow the building to begin. Except for Ulrich, who was still staring dreamily at the drawing. The residents had gone through every major concern possible, but were now nit-picking over trivial details. No one wanted to end the discussion on the biggest thing to happen in Edelweiss since Olga Beamesderfer had had triplets. "If you all would excuse me, I have some pressing business that needs my attention. My assistant, Chad Wenrich, will answer your remaining questions."

He handed Chad the mike and walked over to Gretchen. He whispered, "Mark your ballot."

"It's not time to vote yet."

"Do it anyway. You have enough information to make an intelligent choice. Besides, you won't be here when the vote is officially counted."

One finely arched brow rose. "I won't?"

Jordon grinned wolfishly. "You're going to be two miles away from here."

"Doing what?"

Jordon's grin widened, and his dark eyebrows danced. Sinful delight was in his smile.

Gretchen quickly marked her ballot, handed it to Erik, and followed Jordon. She ignored the stares and questioning looks they received as they squeezed passed the standing-room-only in the back of the hall. Jordon stopped at the coatroom and got her red cape and his jacket.

She was still buttoning her cape as Jordon ushered her outside. There stood Zelda and the Dragon's Lair sleigh. Gunter was impatiently holding the reins. Jordon helped Gretchen up and then followed her onto the bench. With a thumbs-up sign to Gunter he clicked the reins and Zelda started to trot down the street, heading out of town.

"Where are we going?" Gretchen asked.

Jordon chuckled and steered Zelda across a field. He was heading for Lake Conquest. "No one will be skating tonight," she said.

"I know." He wasn't surprised she figured out where they were headed.

"There won't be any bonfires."

"I know that too." He smiled into the night. The

weather had cooperated perfectly with his plans. It was in the high twenties with no wind, a virtual heat wave for New Hampshire in the middle of winter.

Gretchen glanced around and absently shrugged. It was a nice night for a sleigh ride. "The council will vote in favor of your hotel."

"Hmmm."

"The Hotel Edelweiss is a stroke of genius. You really did find the middle ground."

"Hmmm."

In exasperation she said, "You don't want to discuss the project, do you?"

"No." Lake Conquest was dead ahead of them.

"What do you want to talk about?"

Jordon could see the glimmer of ice in the distance. Somewhere around here was the secluded shelter of trees Gunter had told him about. He spotted it to his left and headed in that direction. "Us."

Gretchen looked at him. He was serious. He was driving them two miles out of town to talk. Was what he was going to say so bad, he was afraid she'll rant and rave loud enough that the entire town would hear her? She noted a pale light shining through the trees and found that odd. As Zelda trotted around a clump of trees, she saw a lantern hanging on a tree illuminating the path into a small clearing.

A gasp of surprise escaped her lips when she saw what was in the clearing. A tent that was lit from within. "What the heck?"

Jordon stopped the sleigh and jumped down. He tied the reins to a nearby tree and fed Zelda a carrot. "I know it's not much, but considering the circumstances it's the best I could come up with." He walked back to the sleigh and picked up a horse blanket. He shook it out and draped it over Zelda's back.

"What circumstances are we talking about here?"

"In case you haven't noticed, it's damn cold in New Hampshire this time of year." He reached up to help her down.

Gretchen frowned but went into his arms. She gasped in wonder as he swung her up and cradled her against his chest.

"One of us with wet feet is enough." He strolled to the tent and, balancing his precious bundle, unzipped the front flap. He bent over and lowered her feet to the nylon-covered ground.

A smile lit up Gretchen's face as she spotted a vase holding two dozen white roses. "You guessed!" She bent over and smelled their fragrance. Her voice was a little sad as she murmured, "They're not going to live long in this cold."

"There's at least another three dozen waiting for you in your apartment." He stepped out of his shoes and socks and went over to where a knapsack lay.

Gretchen cocked an eyebrow as Jordon rummaged inside it. It was filled with clothes. She saw a pair of her jeans in there. "Are we planning on staying?"

Jordon jammed his freezing feet into a pair of dry socks. "For however long it takes."

She noticed a small ice chest and two thermos bottles sitting in a corner. Black satin pillows were arranged on a double sleeping bag that was spread out in the middle of the tent, taking most of the room. She pulled off her boots and sat down next to Jordon on the down-filled bag. "For what?"

He unzipped his jacket and leaned back on his

elbows. His smile screamed, *Wolf!* "For you to seduce me."

Understanding finally dawned. "You do realize this is Lake Conquest?"

"I wouldn't be out here for any other reason."

She unbuttoned her cape and removed her gloves. Her fingers inched over his knee. "Say it."

Jordon swallowed as her fingers moved higher and teased the inside of his thigh. "Say what?"

Her fingers stopped their ascent.

Jordon reached out and tenderly cupped her chilled cheeks. "I, Jordon Winters, love you, Gretchen Horst." Her brilliant smile added a special glow in the tent. He kissed her mouth and laid down on the sleeping bag. "Now, hurry up and seduce me, so that we can go back into town in disgrace. Every shotgun in town will be pulled out of mothballs and I will be forced to wed the spinster—" Her fingers dug into his thigh. He cleared his throat and tried again, "—I mean sexy innkeeper, and we will live happily ever after."

Gretchen removed her cape and grinned like one of the mountain predators she was so leery of. "You, Mr. Winters, will be so seduced that you will be enslaved to me for life."

Jordon savored the feel of Gretchen's curves as she wiggled her way up his prone body. He captured her mouth in a heated kiss and whispered against her lips, "I already am, love. I already am."

Gretchen snuggled deeper into the bag and against Jordon's warmth. She smiled into the mat of curls covering his chest as he tightened his hold. She wasn't sure who had seduced whom, but she wasn't complaining. "Lord, it was cold out there."

Jordon chuckled. "I didn't plan on doing it on top of the sleeping bag, love. Someone got carried away, as usual."

Gretchen yanked on a tuft of hair.

"Ouch! That hurt." He rubbed the sore spot. "Okay, I take full responsibility for getting carried away."

She kissed the spot he had been rubbing. "That's better."

Jordon felt her lips against his chest and sighed. He slid a leg in between hers. Contentment, satisfaction, and love glowed within the small boundaries of the blue nylon tent.

After several minutes he whispered, *"Liebchen?"*

Gretchen raised her head. "You've picked up some German.

"Gunter has taught me only one word so far. I figured I'd better learn it if I want to know what everyone is saying around here."

"I'm so happy we'll be staying in Edelweiss, Jordon. I would have moved anywhere to be with you, though."

He kissed her forehead and pressed her head back down on his chest. "I know, love." He cleared his throat and stared up at the nylon ceiling. "I can only foresee one slight problem in our future."

"What?" she murmured.

"I might need some tips on how to manage the hotel."

Gretchen's laughter rang in the small clearing. Zelda opened one eye and snorted her disapproval at being awakened at such an ungodly hour.

Epilogue

Jordon admired the view of his wife's jean-clad bottom in front of him as he climbed the southern slope of Thunder Mountain. Being married for the past three months to Gretchen was the best thing that ever happened to him. His desire had grown daily, along with his love. "Are we almost there yet?"

Gretchen turned around and wiped a sleeve of her flannel shirt across her brow. She smiled as her husband joined her. "It's right around the bend."

He followed her to a rocky ledge and wrapped his arms around her waist as they admired the view. Edelweiss laid in peaceful serenity below. Spring had arrived, bringing with it fragrant grass, an abundance of flowers, and, regrettably, heat that melted the snow. The peaks of Shadow and Thunder mountains still held their white caps, though, but the valley below was carpeted in green.

"Do you see it?"

Jordon looked below and spotted the orange dots that must be the surveyor's flags for the Hotel Edelweiss. By this time next year it would be completed, and tourists would be busily enjoying springtime in New Hampshire. "There's nothing to see yet, *liebchen*."

Gretchen followed his glance. "I'm not talking about Hotel Edelweiss." She leaned her head back and examined the heavens. "What have you been going crazy looking for?"

He squinted as he searched the blue skies. "The dragon you swear is in the inn."

"It's definitely *in* the inn. In fact it's built right into it."

Jordon narrowed his eyes and focused on the Dragon's Lair. He sucked in his breath as the sun moved from behind a cloud and flooded the valley with brilliant light. There on the roof of the inn was a dragon. To be more precise it was the roof. Gretchen had had the entire back roof built with different-colored slates to look like a dragon. Red and green slates glistened under the sunlight, but the amber-colored eye gleamed fire. "Lord, Gretchen, he's magnificent. What did you use for the eye?"

"It's a quartz crystal called citrine."

He wished he had brought a pair of binoculars to study it more closely. The dragon was invisible from Shadow Mountain, but from this height on Thunder Mountain it was clearly visible. Jordon looked up and studied the snow-capped peak of Thunder Mountain. If a dragon lived in the upper reaches of the mountain, he would look down and clearly see the dragon below. Since dragons were solitary creatures and never bothered one another, the Dragon's Lair would be safe from any wayward dragons looking for an easy meal. The mountain predators would stay away. Gretchen had protected her inn the same way she protected herself while she slept, with a dragon.

His arms tightened around the woman who held his heart and would, he hoped, one day carry his child. He understood what she was doing. When fighting fire, use fire. When fighting dragons, use dragons. "Do you think Hotel Edelweiss would look good with a dragon on its roof?"

Tears pooled in her eyes as she flung her arms around her husband's neck. "I thought you'd never ask."

THE EDITOR'S CORNER

What a marvelously exciting time we'll have next month, when we celebrate LOVESWEPT's ninth anniversary! It was in May 1983 that the first LOVESWEPTs were published, and here we are, still going strong, still as committed as ever to bringing you only the best in category romances. Several of the authors who wrote books for us that first year have become *New York Times* bestselling authors, and many more are on the verge of achieving that prestigious distinction. We are proud to have played a part in their accomplishments, and we will continue to bring you the stars of today—and tomorrow. Of course, none of this would be possible without you, our readers, so we thank you very much for your continued support and loyalty.

We have plenty of great things in store for you throughout the next twelve months, but for now, let the celebration begin with May's lineup of six absolutely terrific LOVESWEPTs, each with a special anniversary message for you from the authors themselves.

Leading the list is Doris Parmett with **UNFINISHED BUSINESS,** LOVESWEPT #540. And there is definitely unfinished business between Jim Davis and Marybeth Wynston. He lit the fuse of her desire in college but never understood how much she wanted independence. Now, years later, fate plays matchmaker and brings them together once more when his father and her mother start dating. Doris's talent really shines in this delightful tale of love between two couples.

In **CHILD BRIDE,** LOVESWEPT #541, Suzanne Forster creates her toughest, sexiest renegade hero yet. Modern-day bounty hunter Chase Beaudine rides the Wyoming badlands and catches his prey with a lightning whip. He's ready for anything—except Annie Wells, who claims they were wedded to each other five years ago when he was in South America on a rescue mission. To make him believe her, Annie will use the most daring—and passionate—

moves. This story sizzles with Suzanne's brand of stunning sensuality.

Once more Mary Kay McComas serves up a romance filled with emotion and fun—**SWEET DREAMIN' BABY**, LOVESWEPT #542. In the small town where Bryce LaSalle lives, newcomers always arouse curiosity. But when Ellis Johnson arrives, she arouses more than that in him. He tells himself he only wants to protect and care for the beautiful stranger who's obviously in trouble, but he soon finds he can do nothing less than love her forever. With her inimitable style, Mary Kay will have you giggling, sighing, even shedding a tear as you read this sure-to-please romance.

Please give a rousing welcome to newcomer Susan Connell and her first LOVESWEPT, **GLORY GIRL**, #543. In this marvelous novel, Evan Jamieson doesn't realize that his reclusive next-door neighbor for the summer is model Holly Hamilton, the unwilling subject of a racy poster for Glory Girl products. Evan only knows she's a mysterious beauty in hiding, one he's determined to lure out into the open—and into his arms. This love story will bring out the romantic in all of you and have you looking forward to Susan's next LOVESWEPT.

Joyce Anglin, who won a Waldenbooks award for First Time Author in a series, returns to LOVESWEPT with **OLD DEVIL MOON**, #544. Serious, goal-oriented Kendra Davis doesn't know the first thing about having fun, until she goes on her first vacation in years and meets dashing Mac O'Conner. Then there's magic in the air as Mac shows Kendra that life is for the living . . . and lips are made for kissing. But could she believe that he'd want her forever? Welcome back, Joyce!

Rounding the lineup in a big way is **T.S., I LOVE YOU**, LOVESWEPT #545, by Theresa Gladden. This emotionally vivid story captures that indefinable quality that makes a LOVESWEPT romance truly special. Heroine T. S. Winslow never forgot the boy who rescued her when she was a teenage runaway, the boy who was her first love.

Now, sixteen years later, circumstances have brought them together again, but old sorrows have made Logan Hunter vow never to give his heart. Theresa handles this tender story beautifully!

Look for four spectacular books on sale this month from FANFARE. First, **THE GOLDEN BARBARIAN,** by best-selling author Iris Johansen—here at last is the long-awaited historical prequel to the LOVESWEPT romances created by Iris about the dazzling world of Sedikhan. A sweeping novel set against the savage splendor of the desert, this is a stunningly sensual tale of passion and love between a princess and a sheik, two of the "founders" of Sedikhan. *Romantic Times* calls **THE GOLDEN BARBARIAN** ". . . an exciting tale . . . The sizzling tension . . . is the stuff which leaves an indelible mark on the heart." *Rendezvous* described it as ". . . a remarkable story you won't want to miss."

Critically acclaimed author Gloria Goldreich will touch your heart with **MOTHERS,** a powerful, moving portrait of two couples whose lives become intertwined through surrogate motherhood. What an eloquent and poignant tale about family, friendship, love, and the promise of new life.

LUCKY'S LADY, by ever-popular LOVESWEPT author Tami Hoag, is now available in paperback and is a must read! Those of you who fell in love with Remy Doucet in **RESTLESS HEART** will lose your heart once more to his brother, for bad-boy Cajun Lucky Doucet is one rough and rugged man of the bayou. And when he takes elegant Serena Sheridan through a Louisiana swamp to find her grandfather, they generate what *Romantic Times* has described as "enough steam heat to fog up any reader's glasses."

Finally, immensely talented Susan Bowden delivers a thrilling historical romance in **TOUCHED BY THORNS.** When a high-born beauty determined to reclaim her heritage strikes a marriage bargain with a daring Irish soldier, she never expects to succumb to his love, a love that would deny the English crown, and a deadly conspiracy.

And you can get these four terrific books only from FANFARE, where you'll find the best in women's fiction.

Also on sale this month in the Doubleday hardcover edition is **INTIMATE STRANGERS** by Alexandra Thorne. In this gripping contemporary novel, Jade Howard will slip into a flame-colored dress—and awake in another time, in another woman's life, in her home . . . and with her husband. Thoroughly absorbing, absolutely riveting!

Happy reading!

With warmest wishes,

Nita Taublib

Nita Taublib
Associate Publisher
FANFARE and LOVESWEPT

FANFARE

NOW On Sale

THE GOLDEN BARBARIAN

☐ (29604-3) $4.99/5.99 in Canada
by Iris Johansen

*"Iris Johansen has penned an exciting tale. . . . The sizzling tension . . . is
the stuff which leaves an indelible mark on the heart."* --<u>Romantic Times</u>
"It's a remarkable tale you won't want to miss." --<u>Rendezvous</u>

MOTHERS

☐ (29565-9) $5.99/6.99 in Canada
by Gloria Goldreich

*The compelling story of two women with deep maternal affection for and
claim to the same child, and of the man who fathered that infant. An
honest exploration of the passion for parenthood.*

LUCKY'S LADY

☐ (29534-9) $4.99/5.99 in Canada
by Tami Hoag

*"Brimming with dangerous intrigue and forbidden passion, this sultry tale
of love . . . generates enough steam heat to fog up any reader's glasses."*
--<u>Romantic Times</u>

TOUCHED BY THORNS

☐ (29812-7) $4.99/5.99 in Canada
by Susan Bowden

*"A wonderfully crafted, panoramic tale sweeping from Yorkshire to Iceland
. . . to . . . London. An imaginative tale that combines authenticity with a
rich backdrop and a strong romance."* -- <u>Romantic Times</u>

THE SYMBOL OF GREAT WOMEN'S
FICTION FROM BANTAM

Ask for these books at your local bookstore or use this page to order.

FN38 - 4/92

FANFARE

On Sale in APRIL

THE FIREBIRDS

☐ 29613-2 $4.99/5.99 in Canada
by Beverly Byrne
author of THE MORGAN WOMEN

The third and final book in Beverly Byrne's remarkable trilogy of passion and revenge. The fortunes of the House of Mendoza are stunningly resolved in this contemporary romance.

FORTUNE'S CHILD

☐ 29424-5 $5.50/6.50 in Canada
by Pamela Simpson

Twenty years ago, Christina Fortune disappeared. Now she's come home to claim what's rightfully hers. But is she an heiress . . . or an imposter?

SEASON OF SHADOWS

☐ 29589-6 $5.99/6.99 in Canada
by Mary Mackey

Lucy and Cassandra were polar opposites, but from the first day they met they became the best of friends. Roommates during the turbulent sixties, they stood beside each other through fiery love affairs and heartbreaking loneliness.

THE SYMBOL OF GREAT WOMEN'S FICTION FROM BANTAM

Ask for these books at your local bookstore or use this page to order.

FN39 - 4/92